Jr
This book belongs to

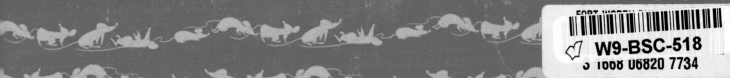

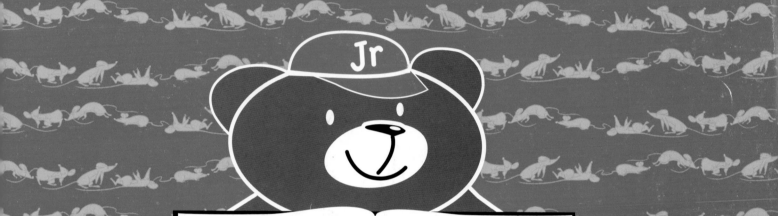

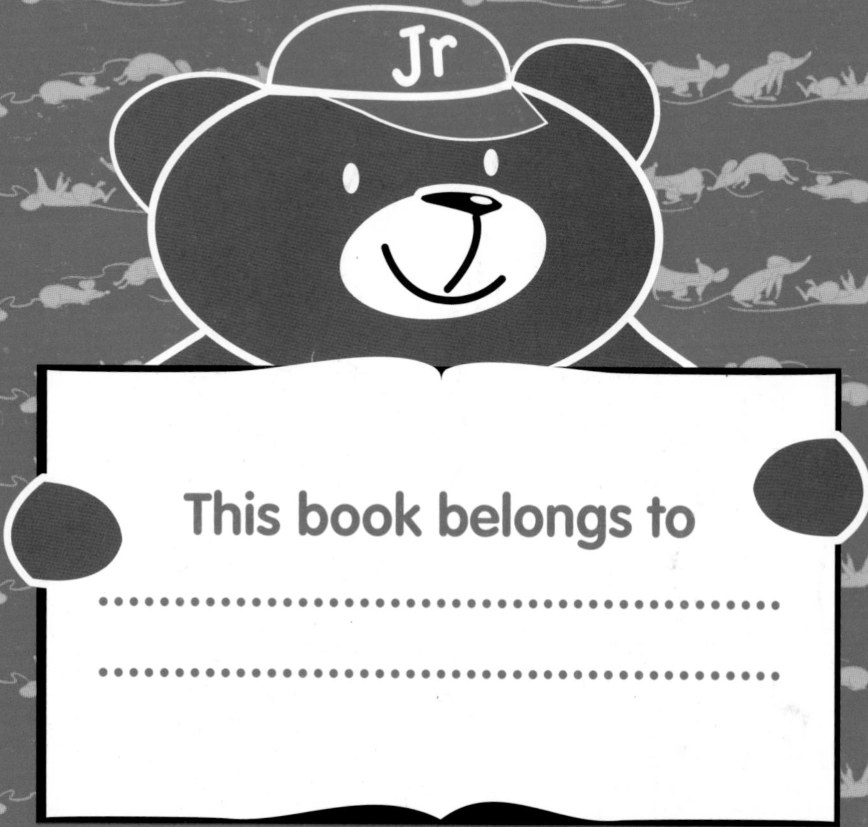

Ganesha
The wonder years

Script
Sourav Dutta

Illustration, Lettering and Design
Rajesh Nagulakonda

Editing
Jason Quinn

Desktop Publishing
Bhavnath Chaudhary

Mission Statement

To entertain and educate young minds by creating unique illustrated books that recount stories of human values, arouse curiosity in the world around us, and inspire with tales of great deeds of unforgettable people.

Published by Kalyani Navyug Media Pvt Ltd
101 C, Shiv House, Hari Nagar Ashram,
New Delhi 110014, India
ISBN: 978-93-81182-10-9

Printed in India

Ganesha
The wonder years

CAMPFIRE™

KALYANI NAVYUG MEDIA PVT LTD

NEW DELHI

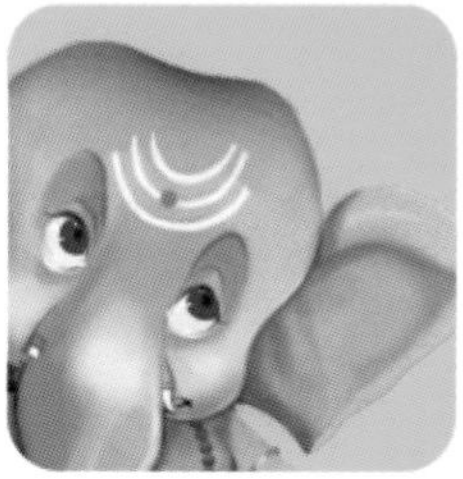

Ganesha

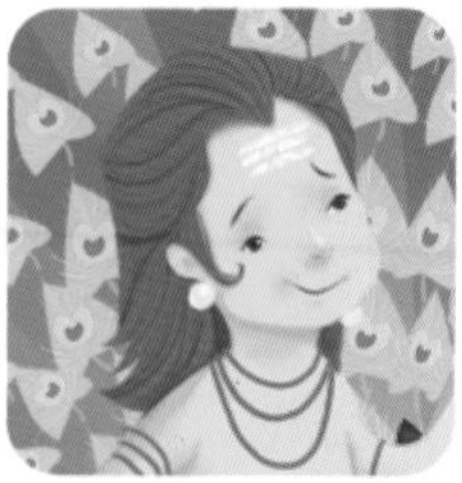

Kartik
Brother

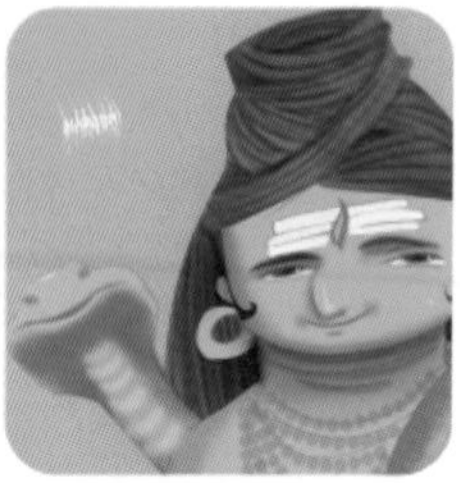

Shiva
Father

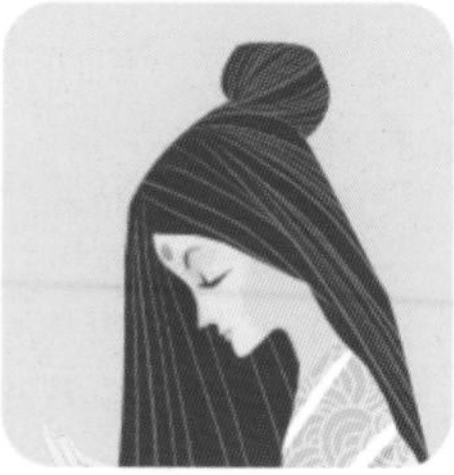

Parvati
Mother

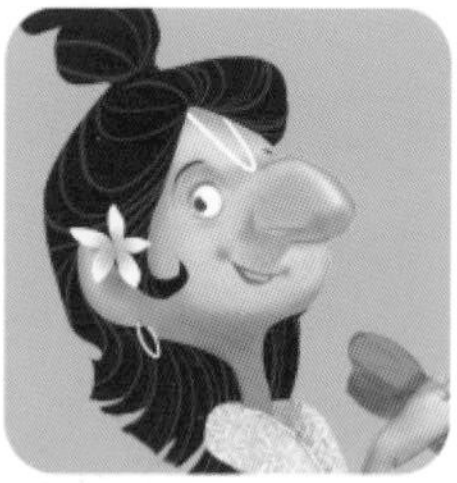

Narada Muni
Traveling Brahmin

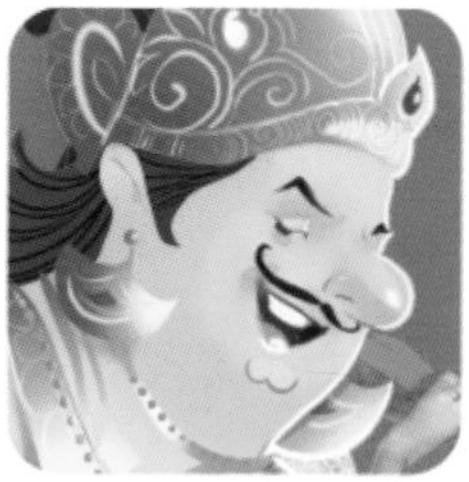

Kubera
Proud Lord of Riches

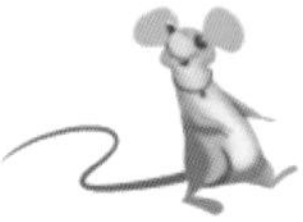

Ganesha and the Big Race

It is morning, and what a fine day!
A fine day for Ganesha and his brother to play.

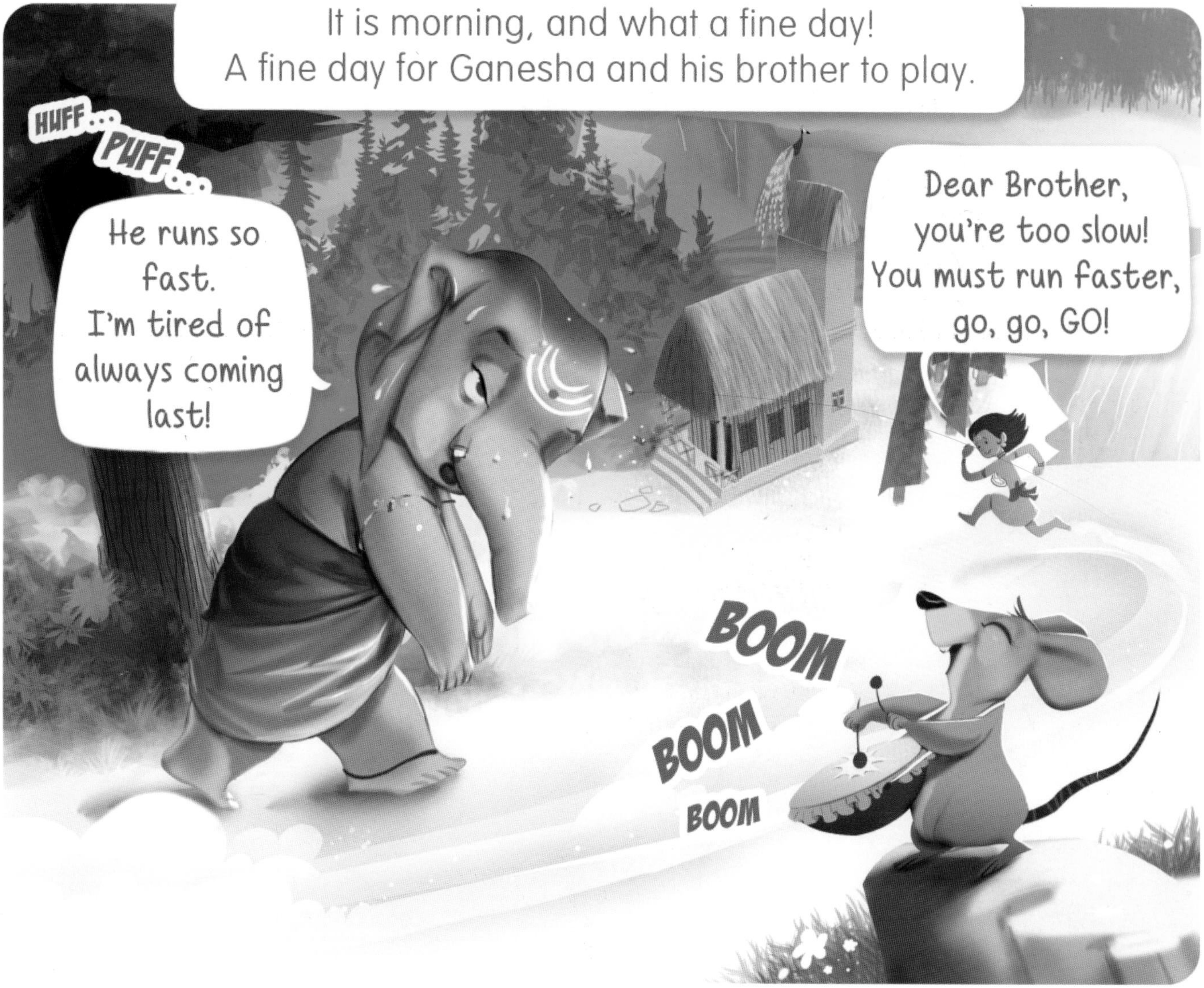
HUFF... PUFF...
He runs so fast. I'm tired of always coming last!
Dear Brother, you're too slow! You must run faster, go, go, GO!
BOOM
BOOM
BOOM

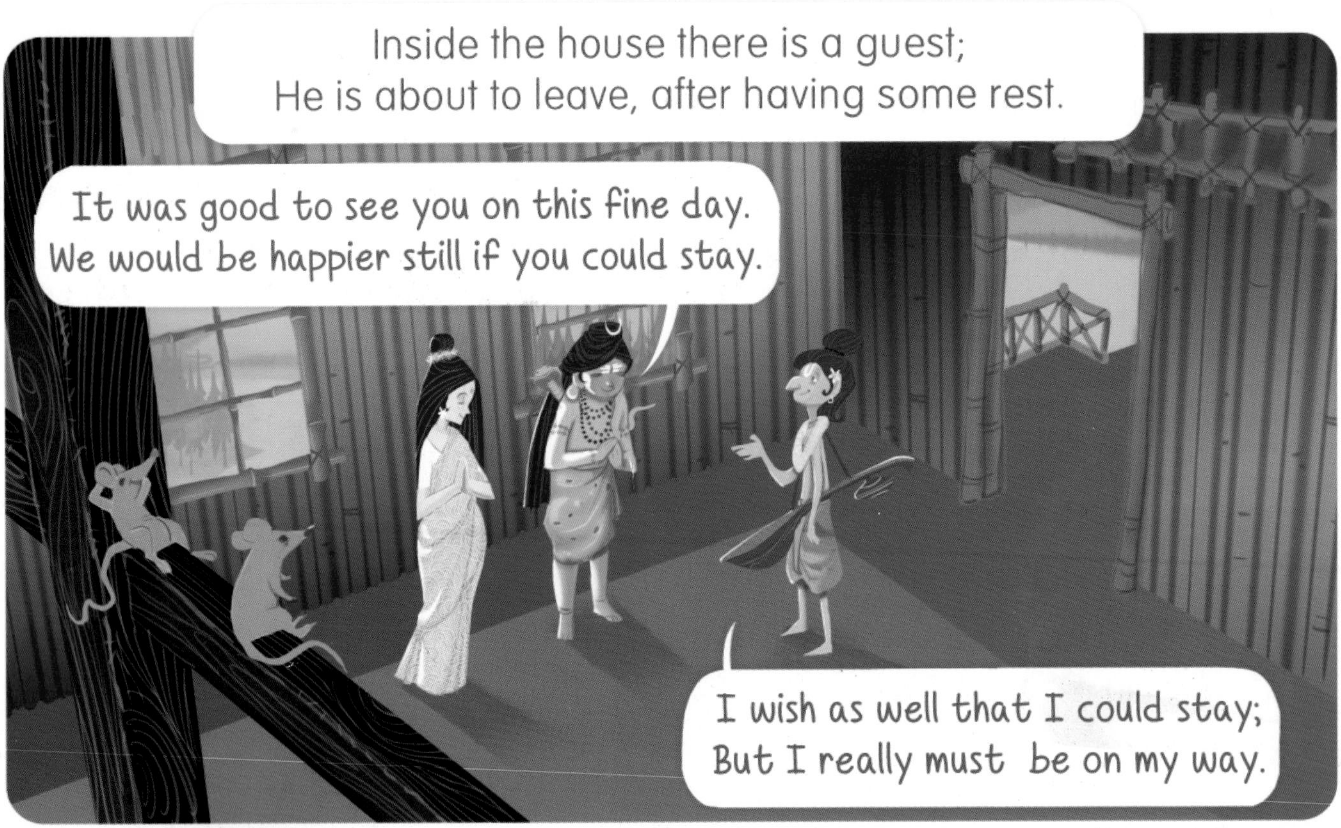
Inside the house there is a guest;
He is about to leave, after having some rest.
It was good to see you on this fine day.
We would be happier still if you could stay.
I wish as well that I could stay;
But I really must be on my way.

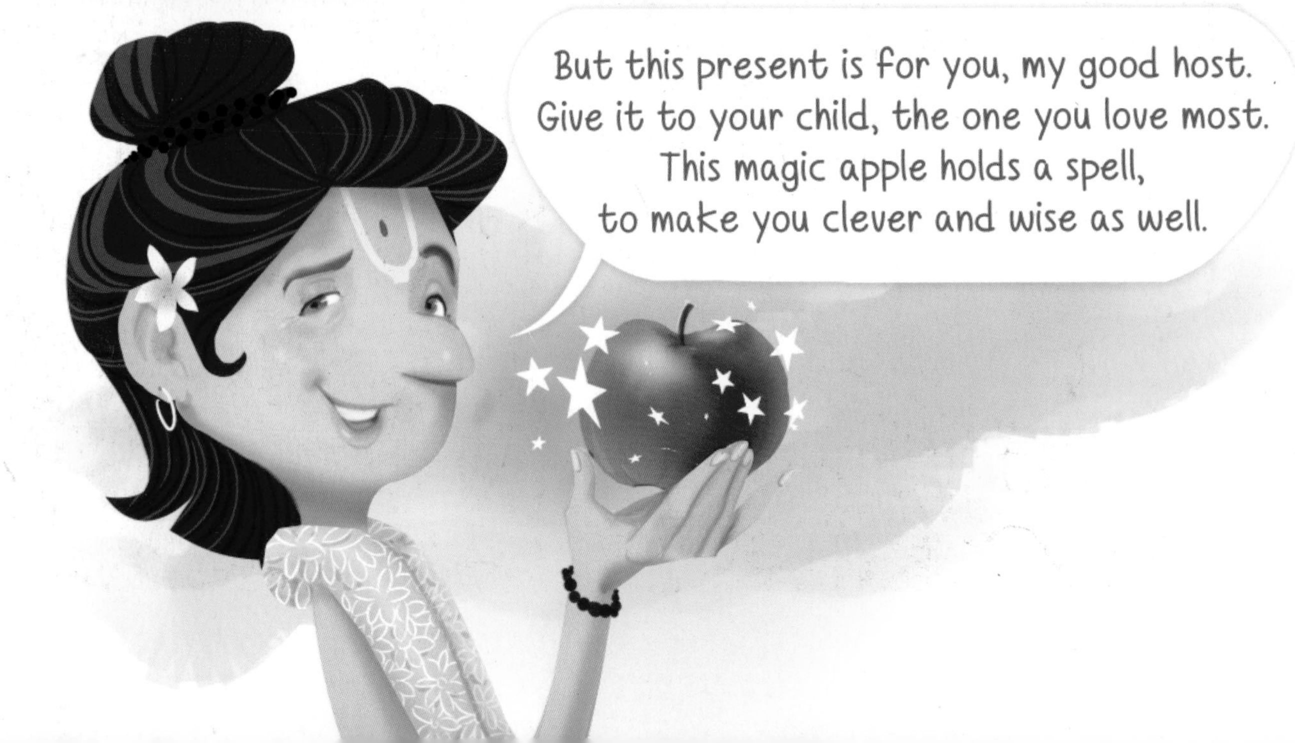
But this present is for you, my good host.
Give it to your child, the one you love most.
This magic apple holds a spell,
to make you clever and wise as well.

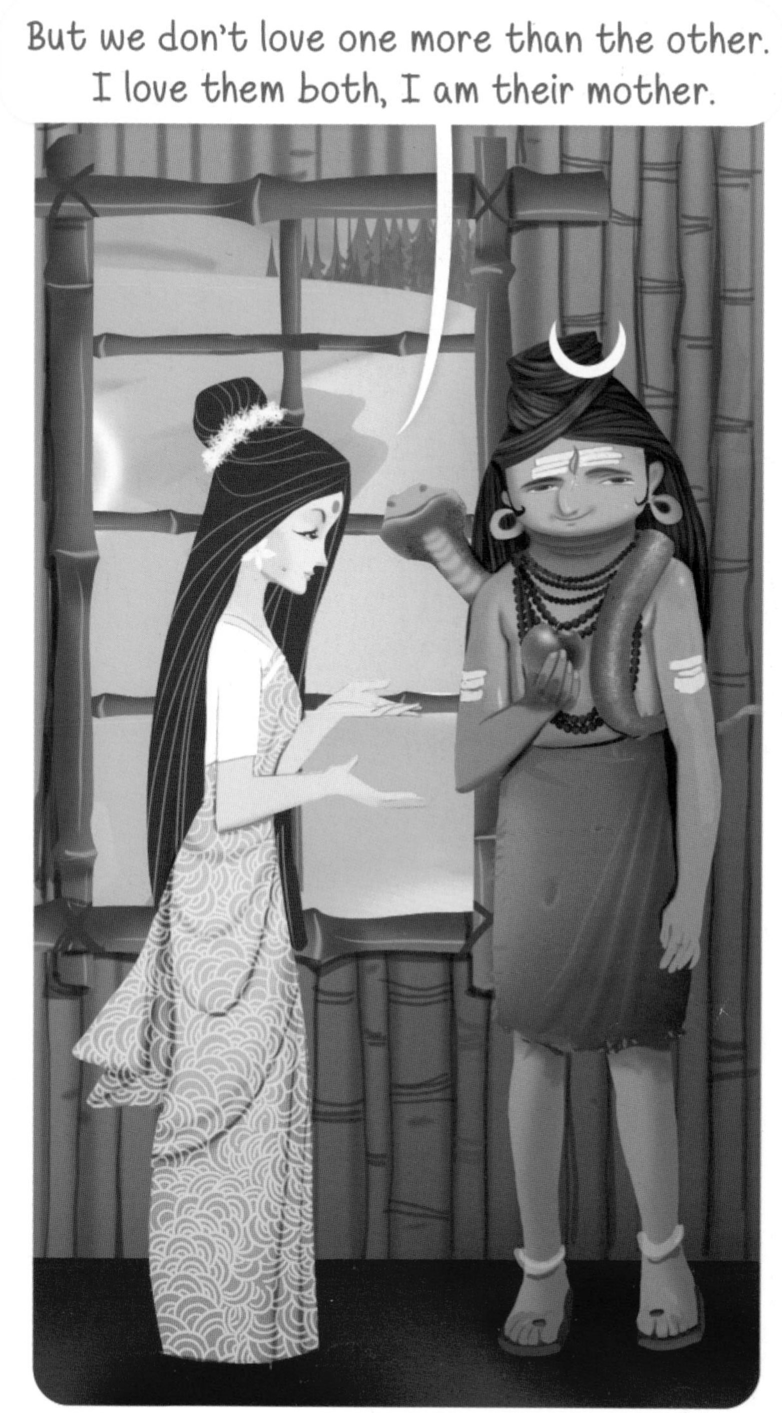
But we don't love one more than the other.
I love them both, I am their mother.
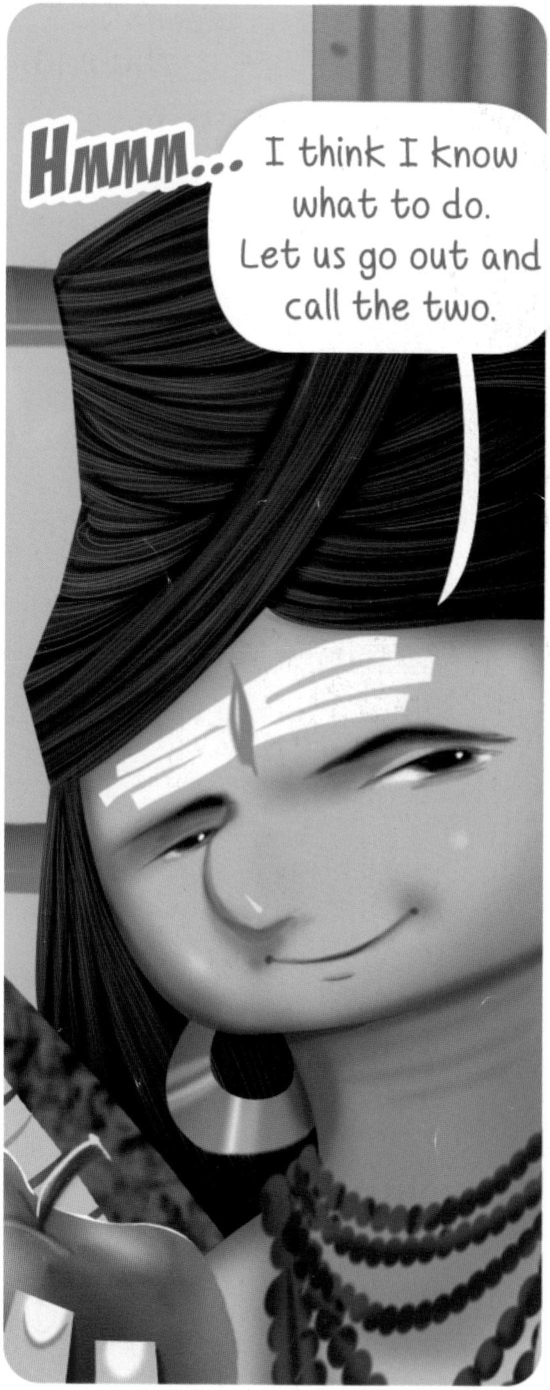
HMMM... I think I know what to do.
Let us go out and call the two.

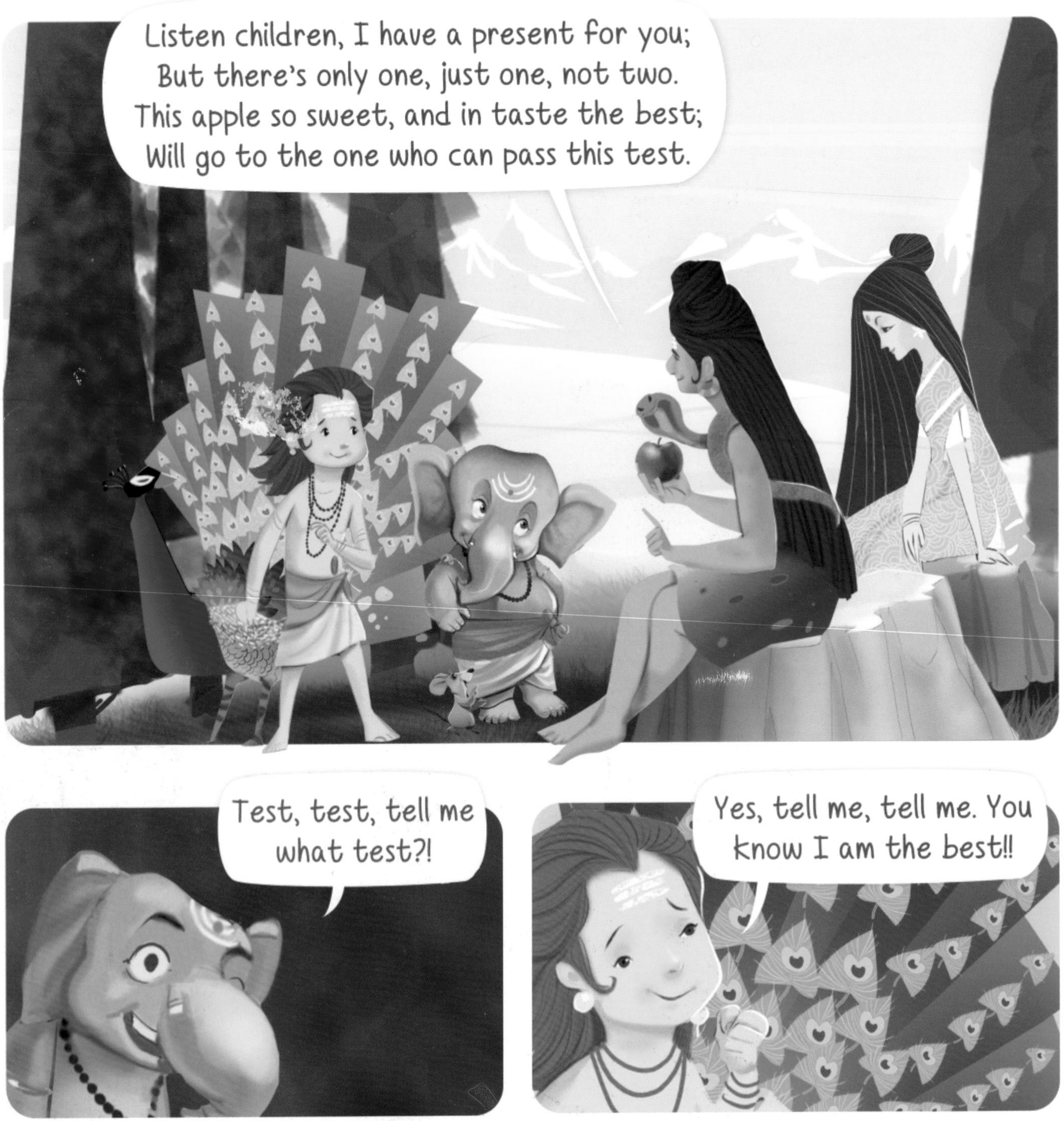
Listen children, I have a present for you;
But there's only one, just one, not two.
This apple so sweet, and in taste the best;
Will go to the one who can pass this test.
Test, test, tell me what test?!
Yes, tell me, tell me. You know I am the best!!

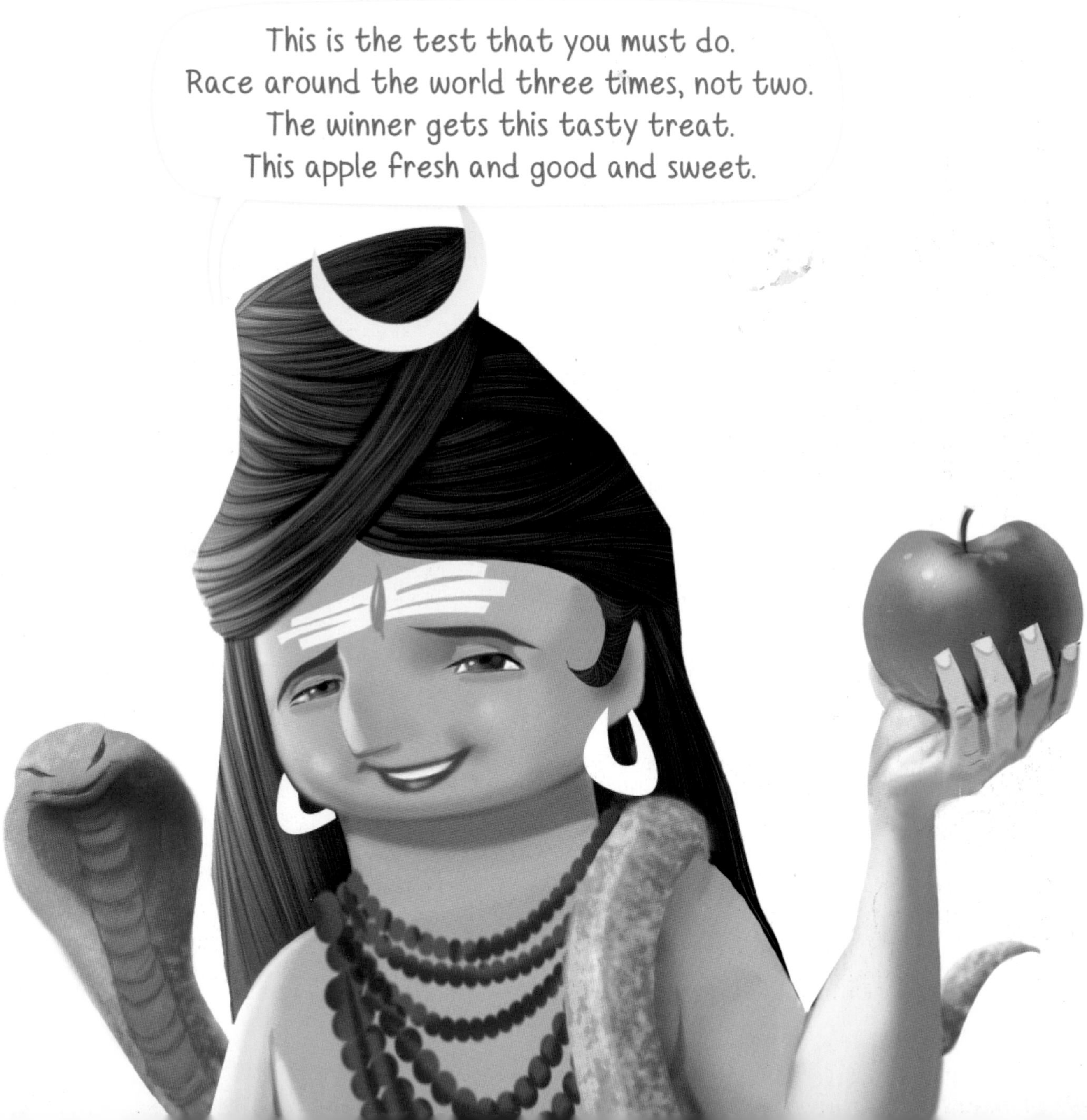
This is the test that you must do.
Race around the world three times, not two.
The winner gets this tasty treat.
This apple fresh and good and sweet.

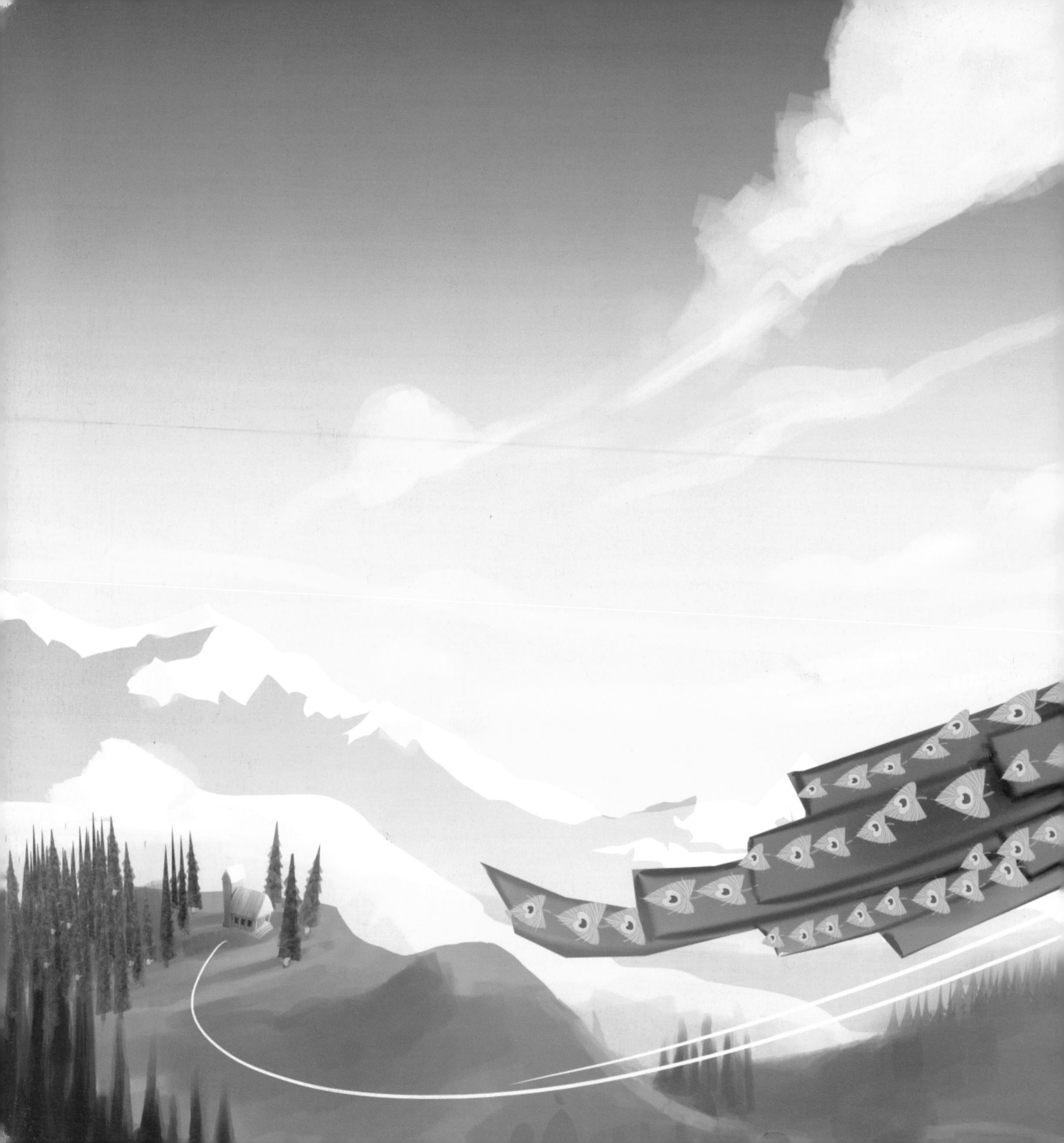

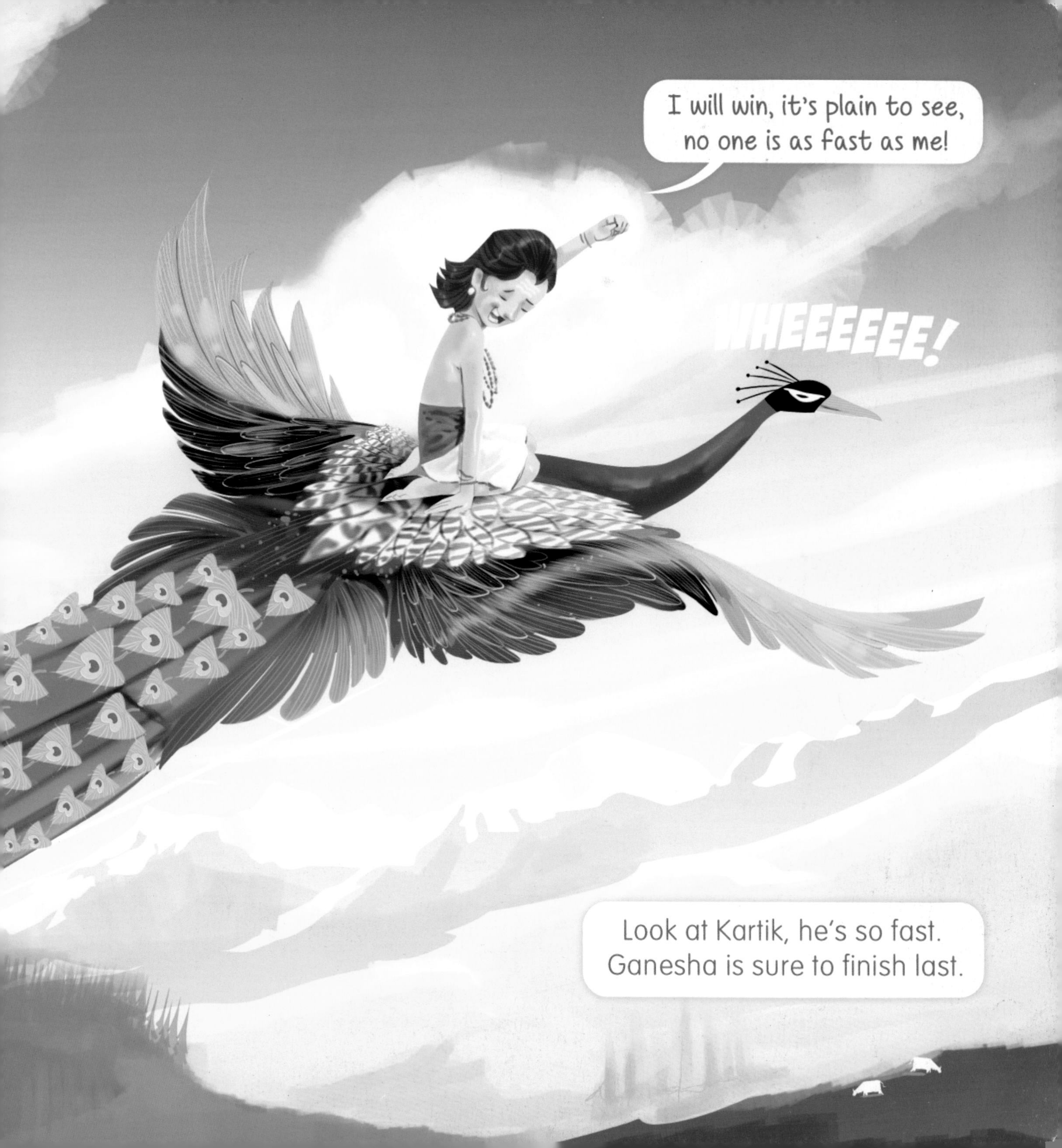
I will win, it's plain to see,
no one is as fast as me!
WHEEEEEE!
Look at Kartik, he's so fast.
Ganesha is sure to finish last.

Look at Ganesha, he is so slow.
He has got a long way to go.

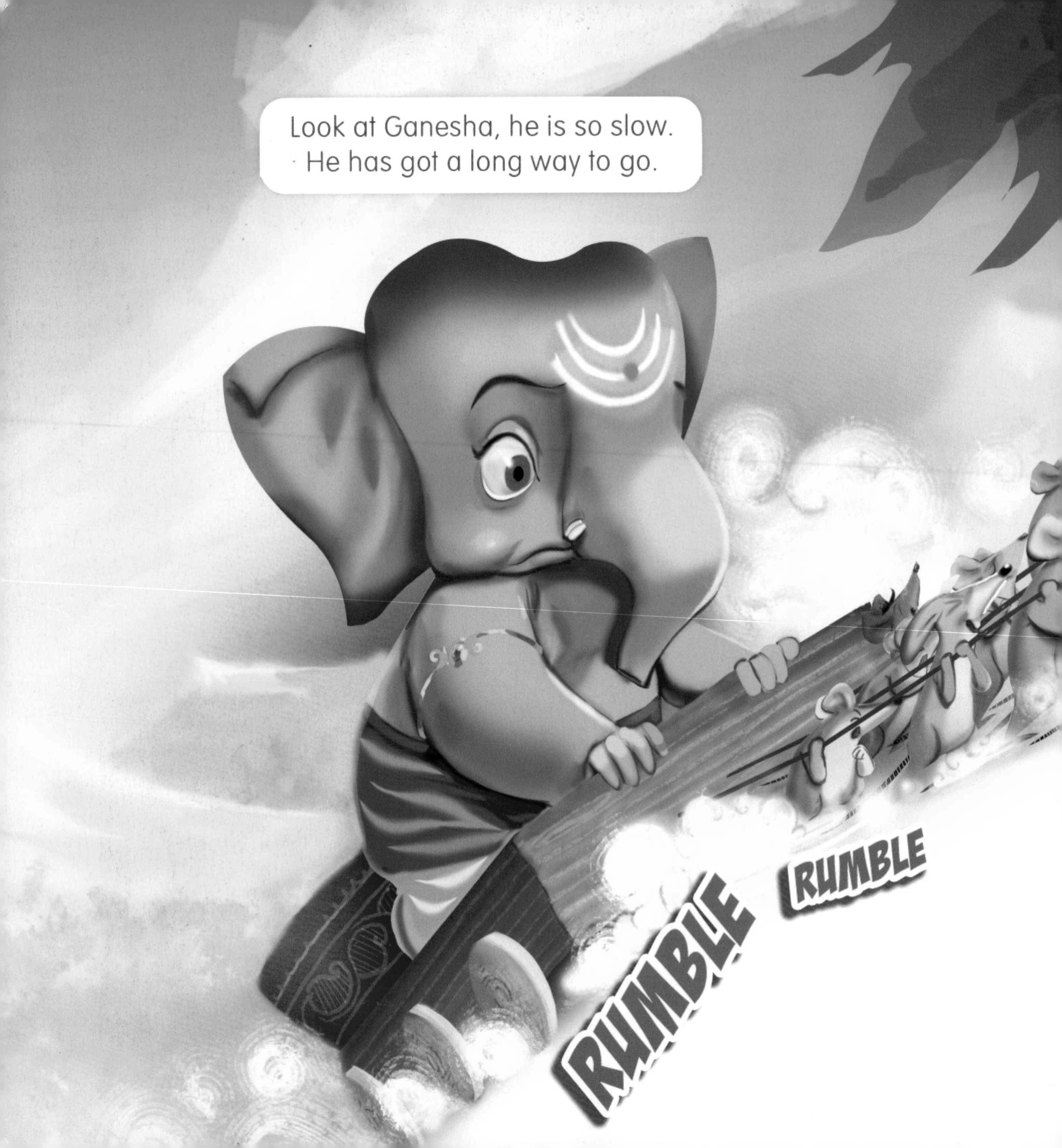
RUMBLE
RUMBLE

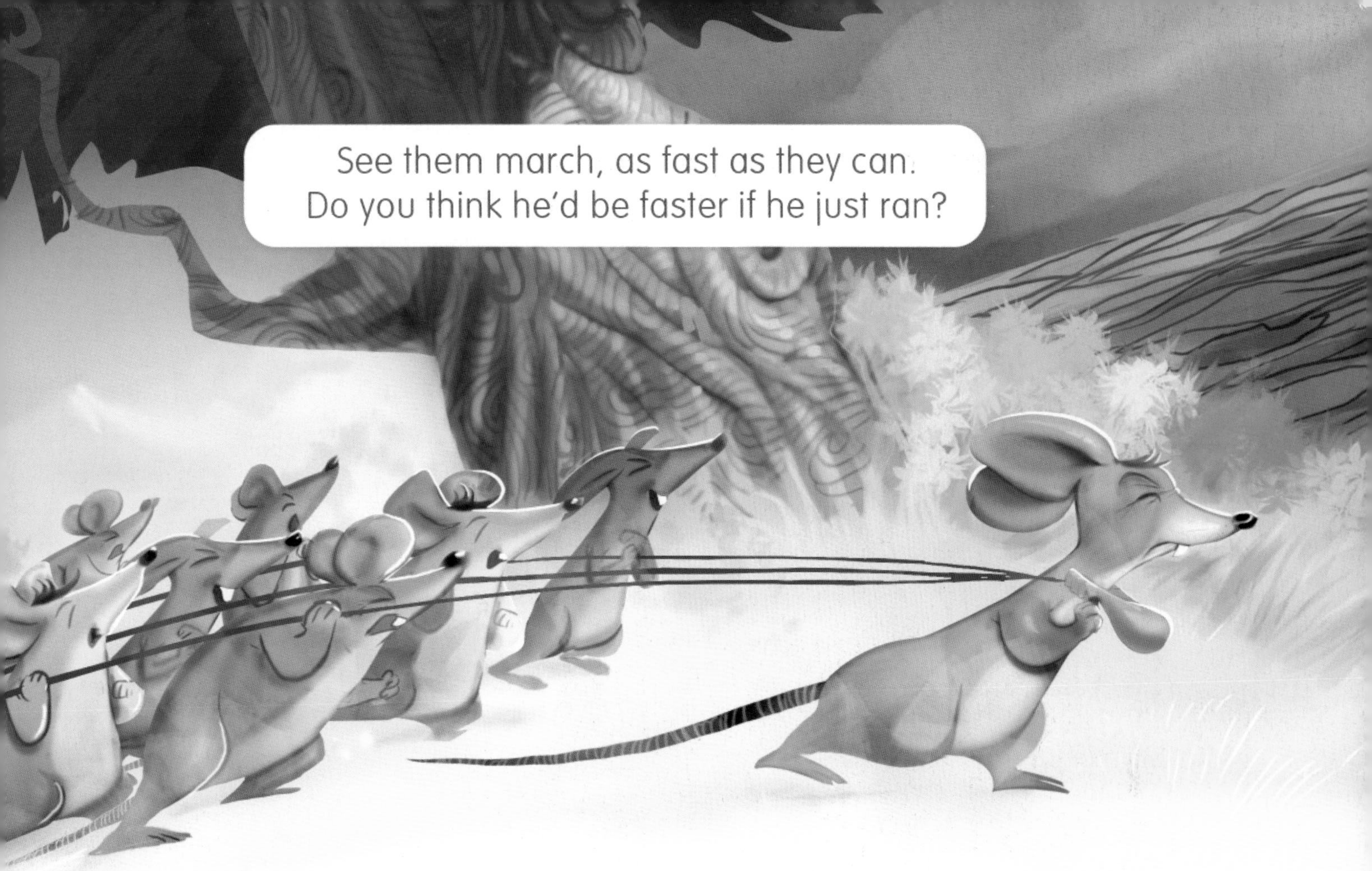
See them march, as fast as they can.
Do you think he'd be faster if he just ran?

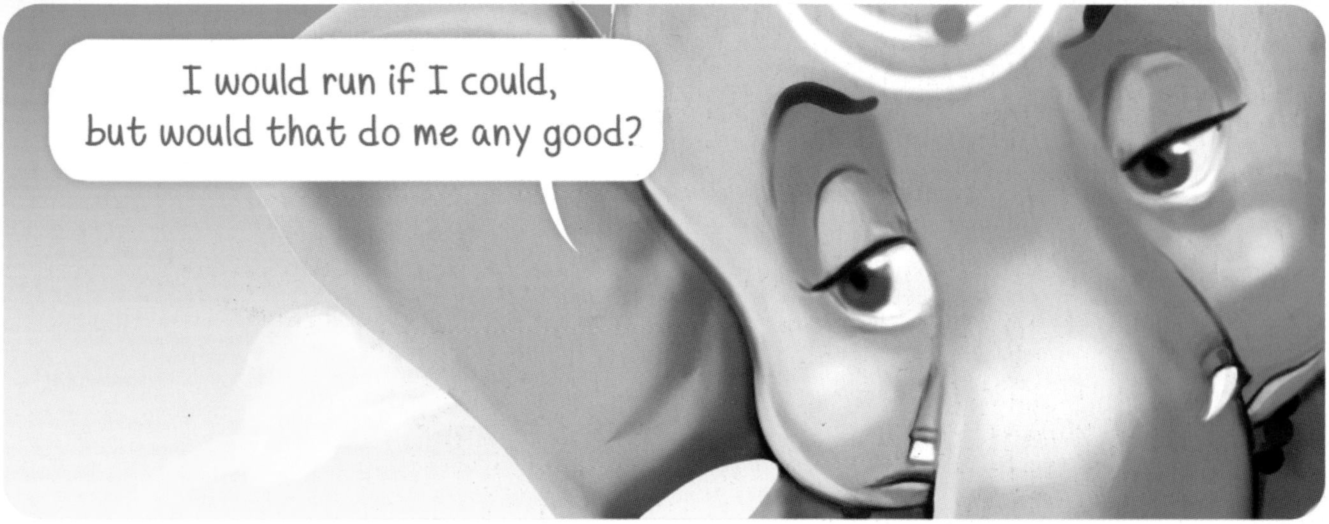
I would run if I could,
but would that do me any good?

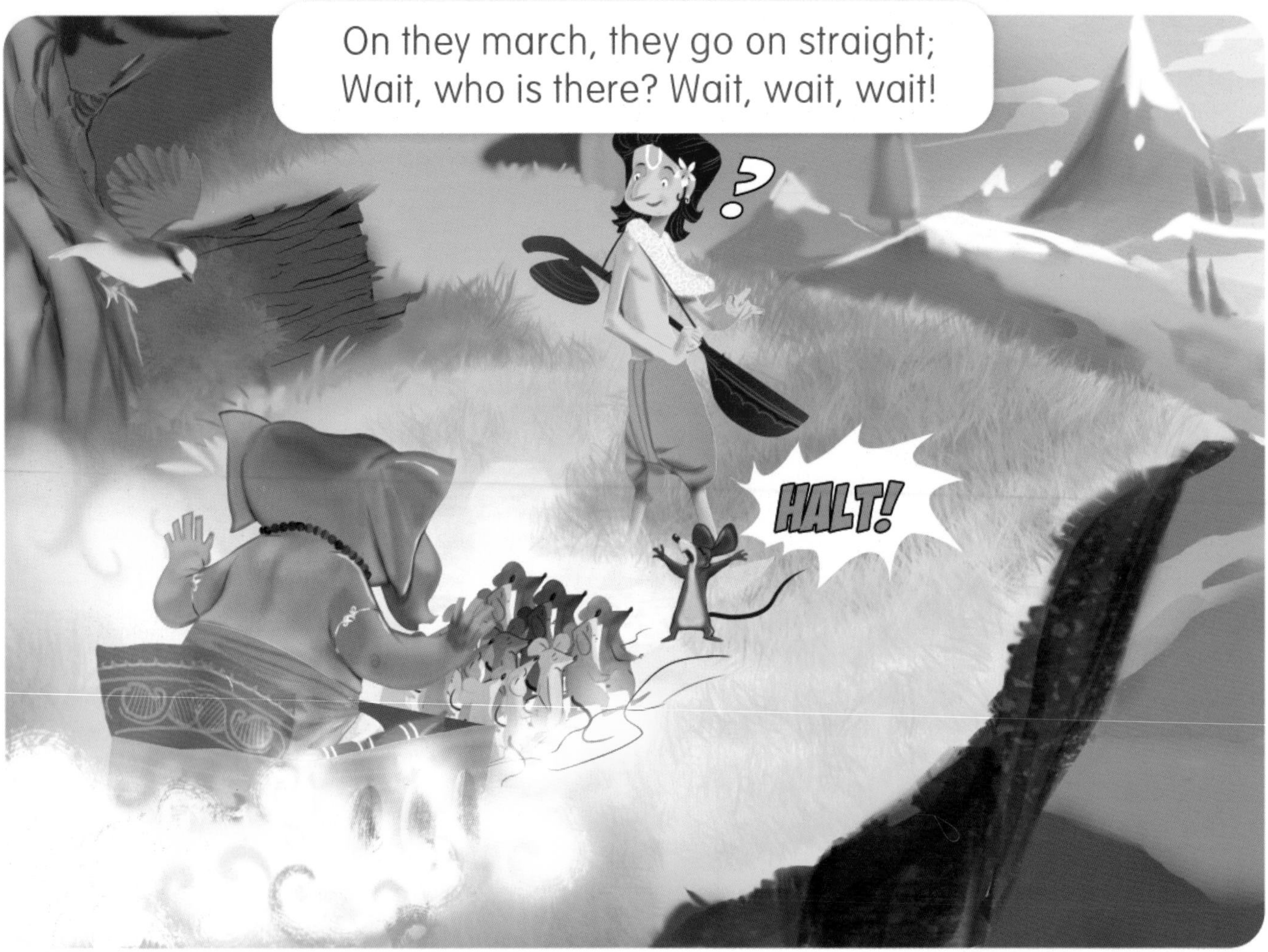
On they march, they go on straight;
Wait, who is there? Wait, wait, wait!
?
HALT!

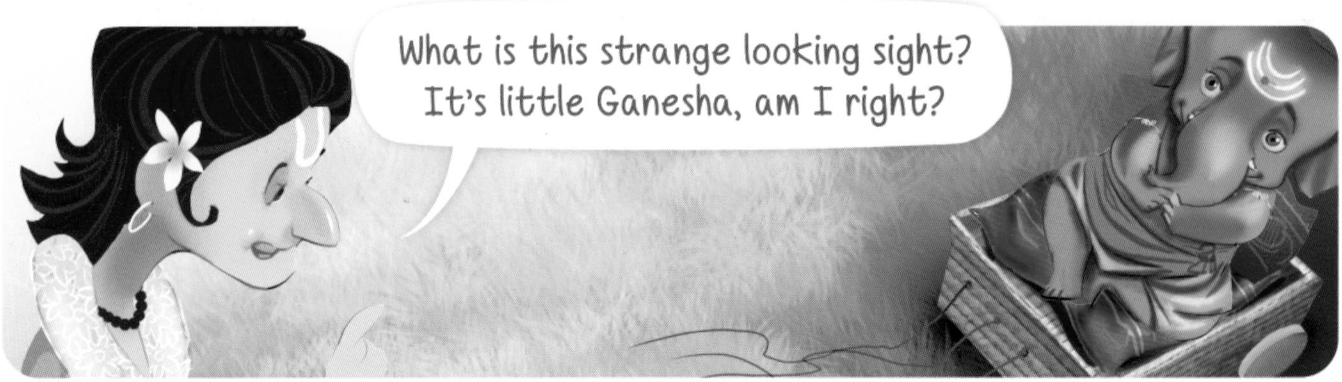
What is this strange looking sight?
It's little Ganesha, am I right?

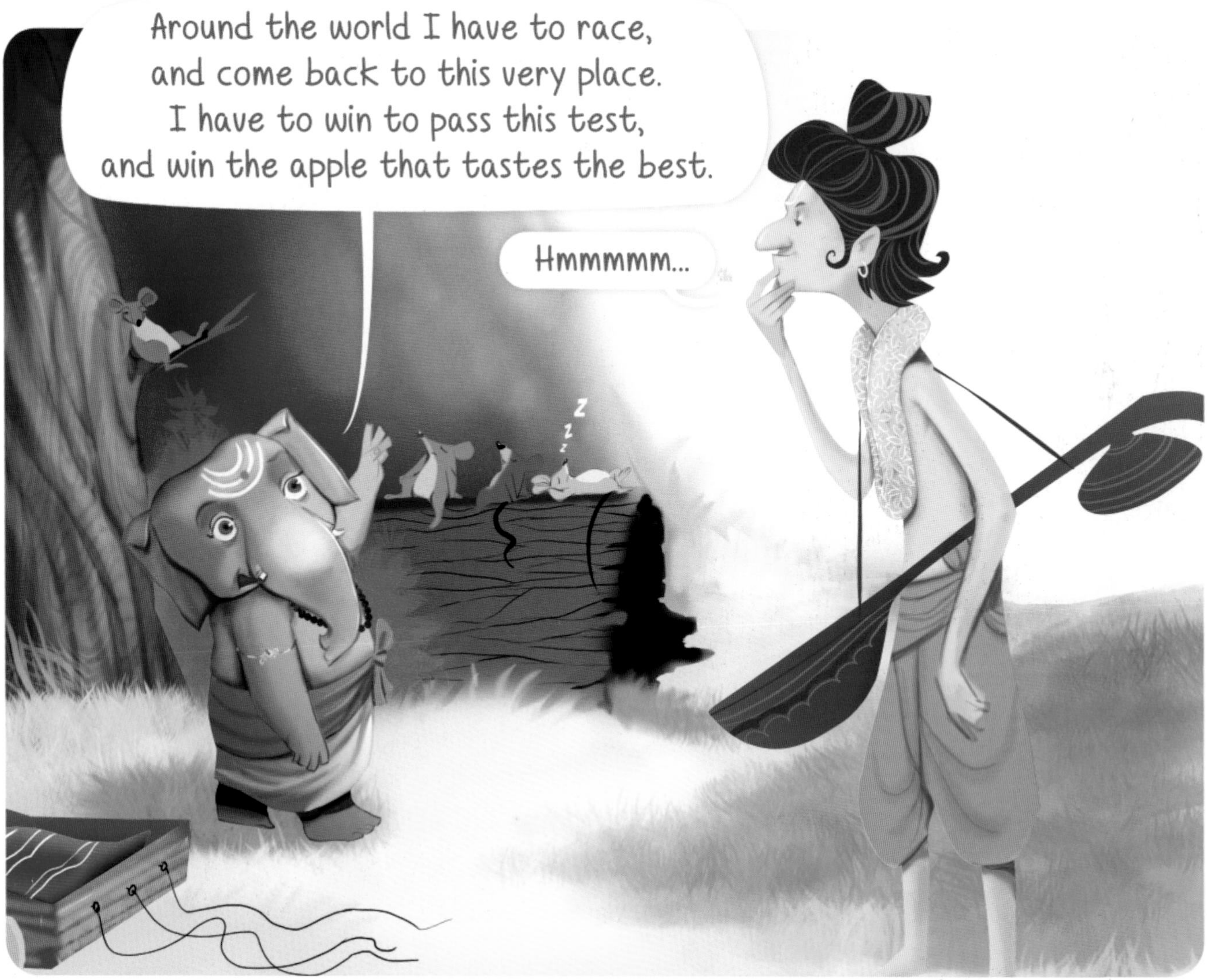
Around the world I have to race,
and come back to this very place.
I have to win to pass this test,
and win the apple that tastes the best.
Hmmmmm...

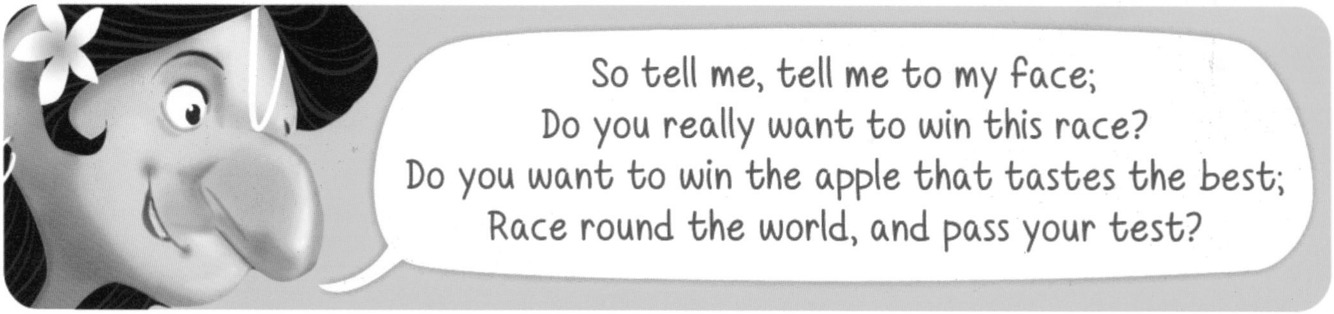
So tell me, tell me to my face;
Do you really want to win this race?
Do you want to win the apple that tastes the best;
Race round the world, and pass your test?

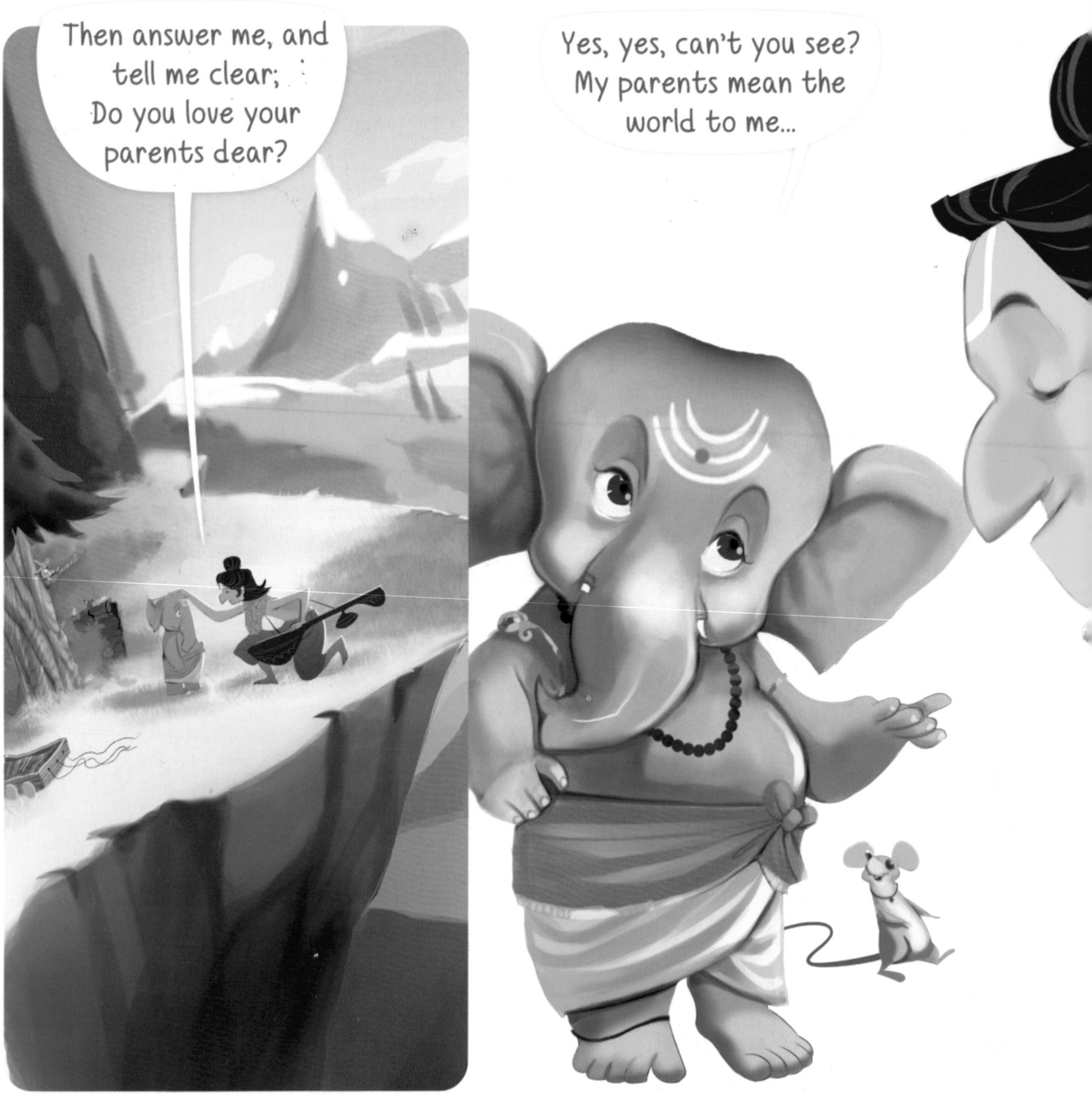
Then answer me, and tell me clear; Do you love your parents dear?
Yes, yes, can't you see? My parents mean the world to me...

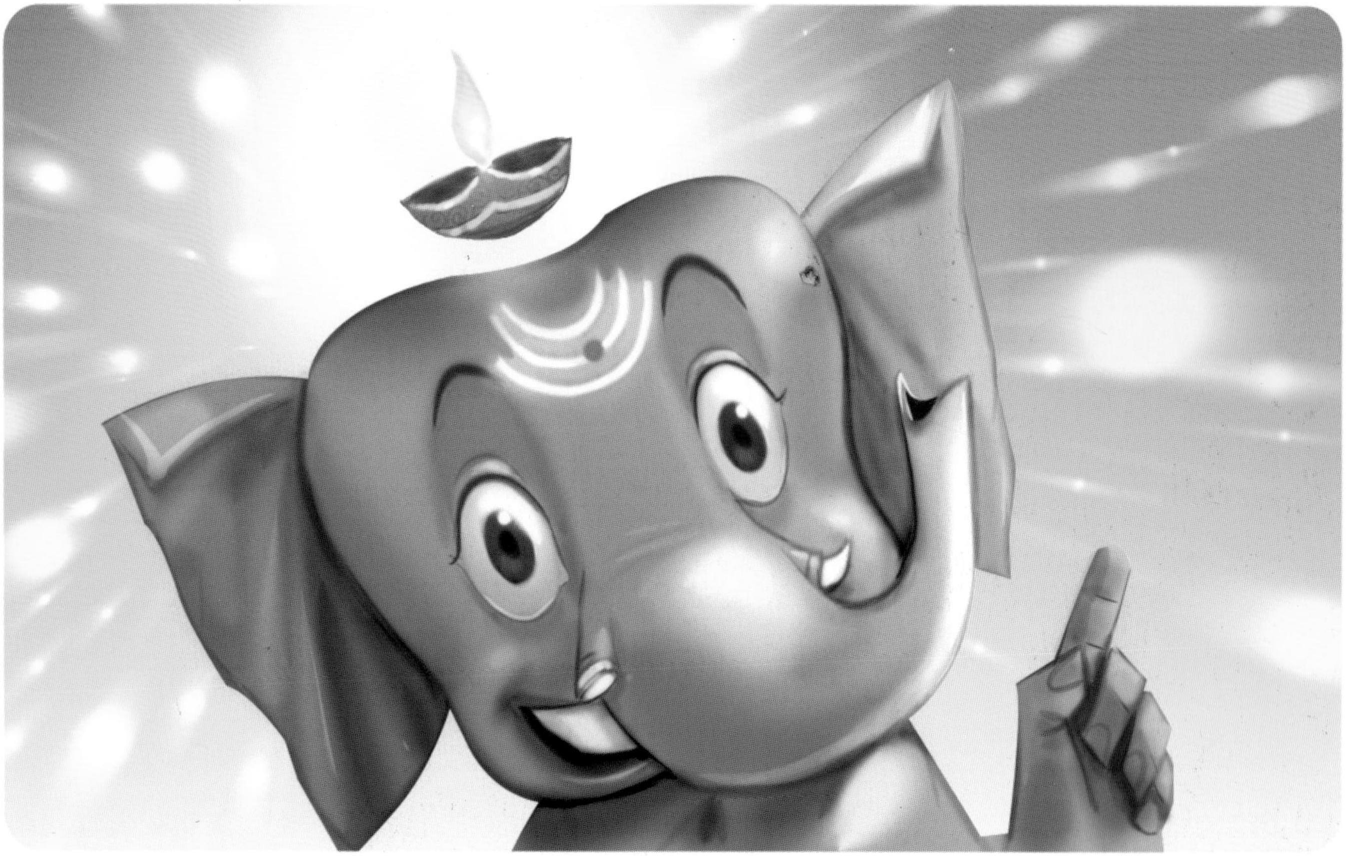

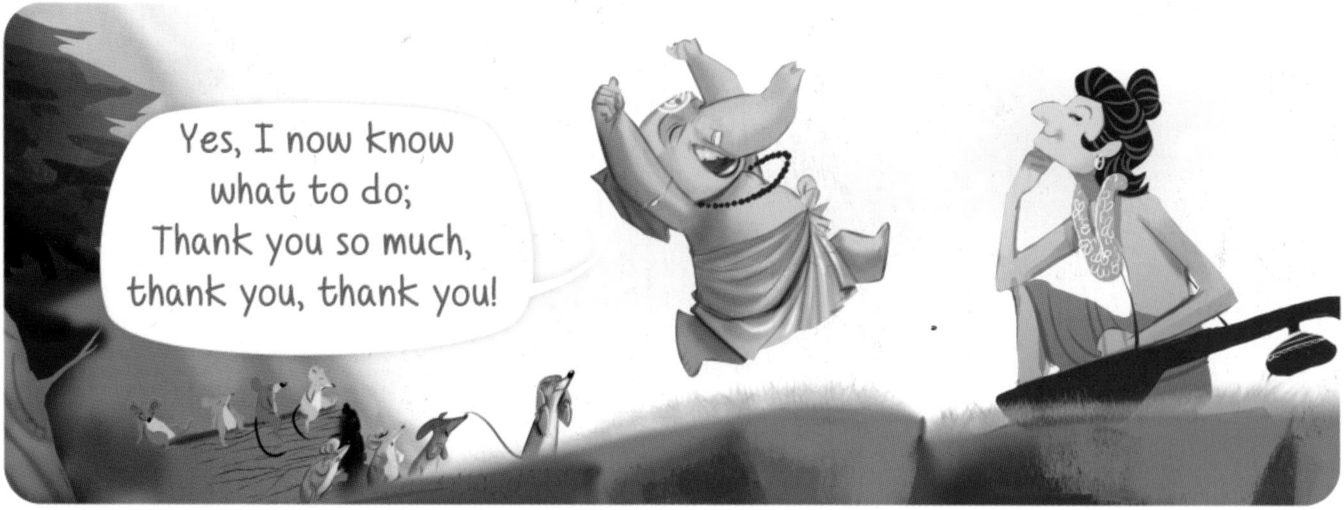
Yes, I now know what to do; Thank you so much, thank you, thank you!

There he goes, just watch him run,
now he's ready for some fun.

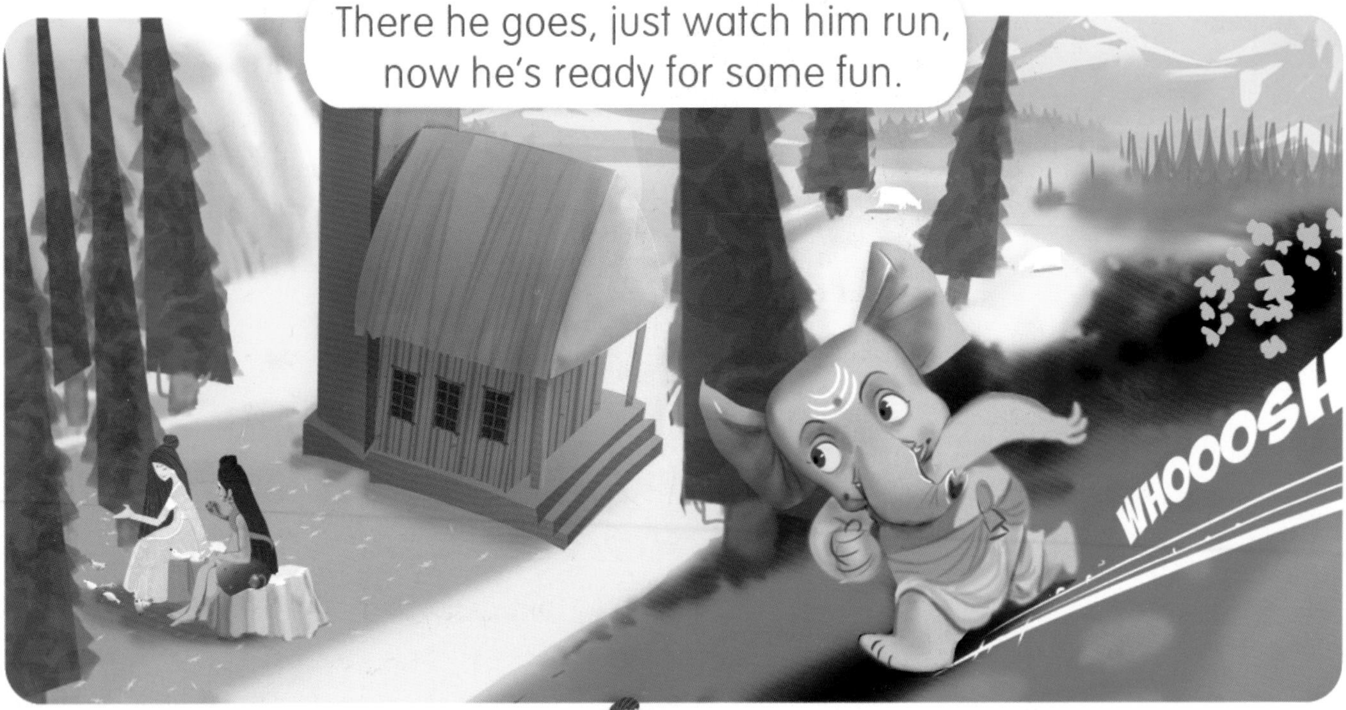
WHOOOSH

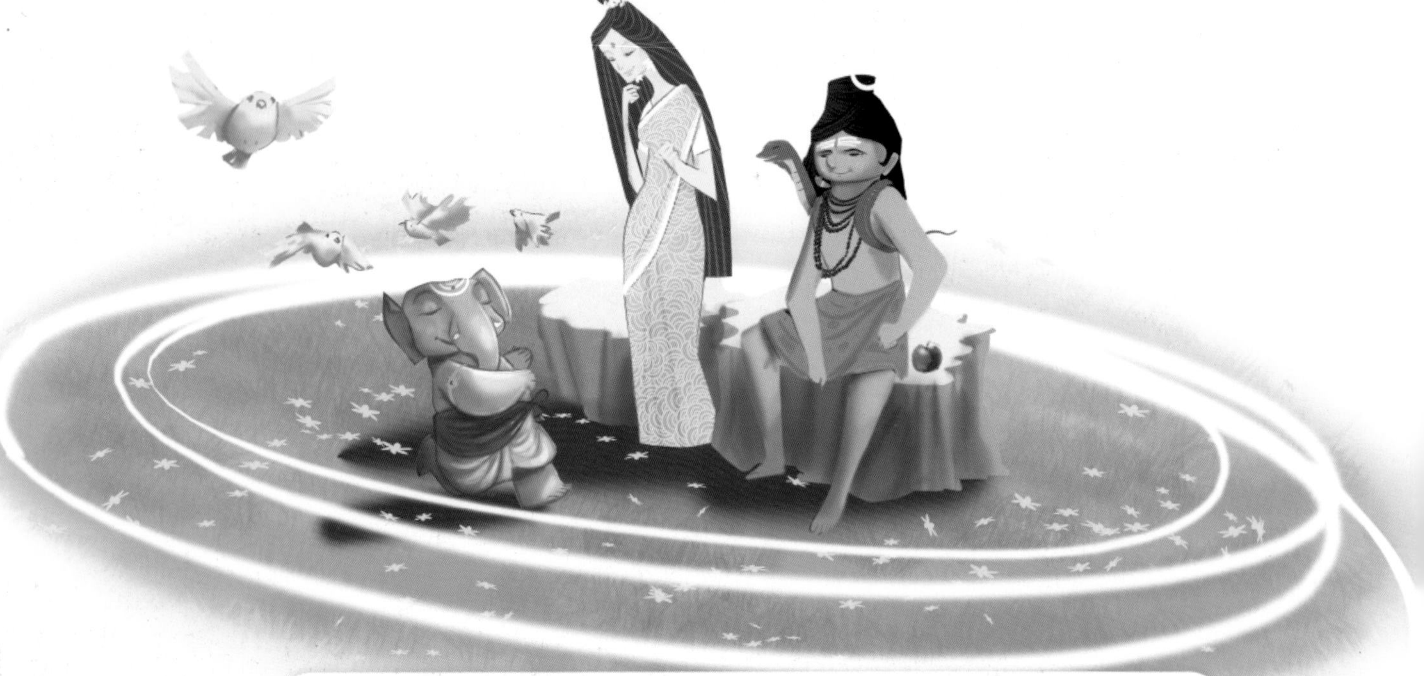

He runs round his parents in circles three;
Can you guess whatever the reason could be?

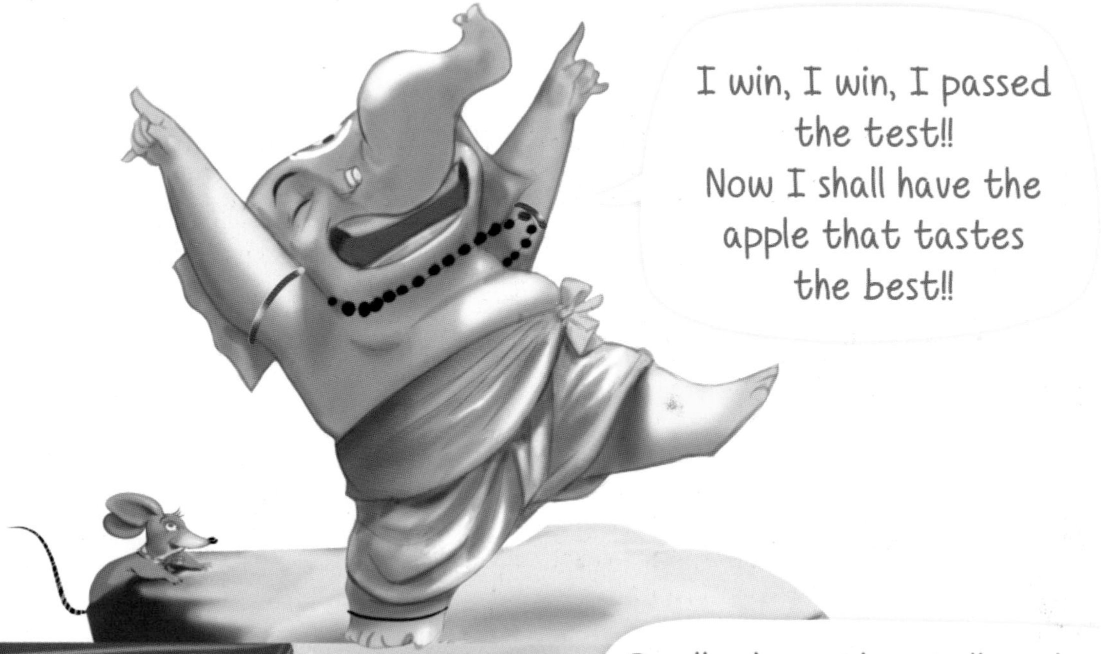
I win, I win, I passed the test!! Now I shall have the apple that tastes the best!!

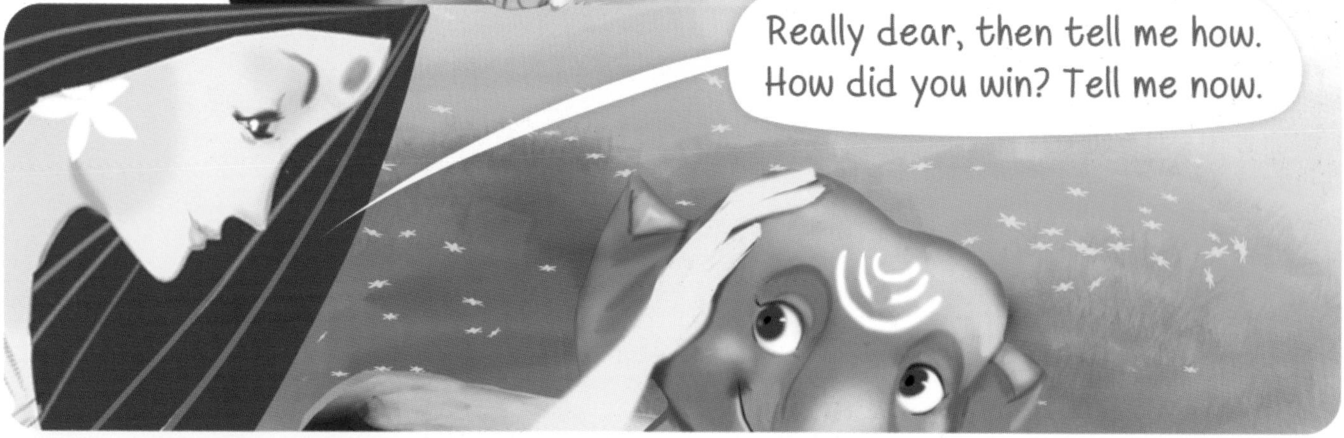
Really dear, then tell me how. How did you win? Tell me now.

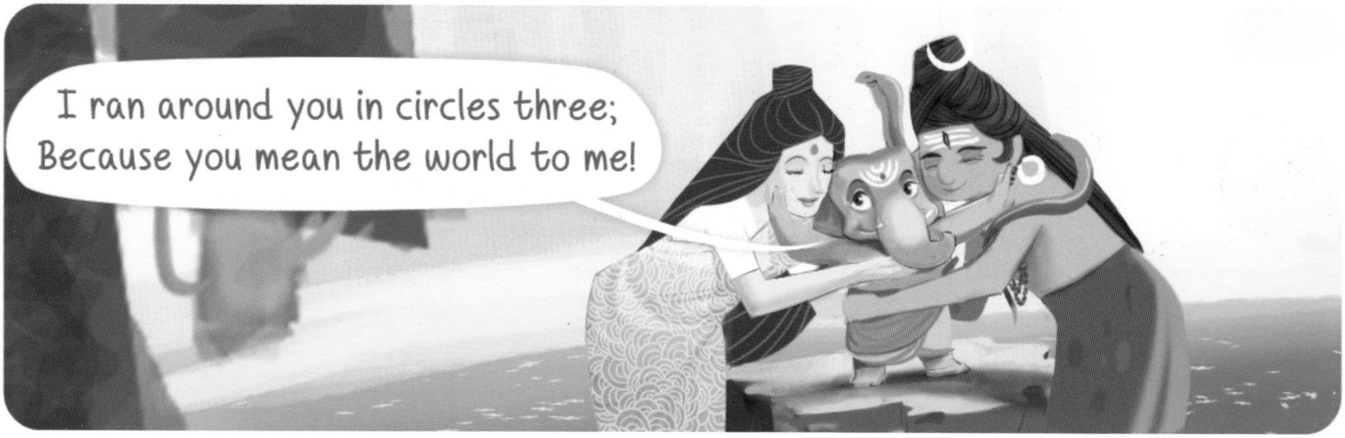
I ran around you in circles three; Because you mean the world to me!

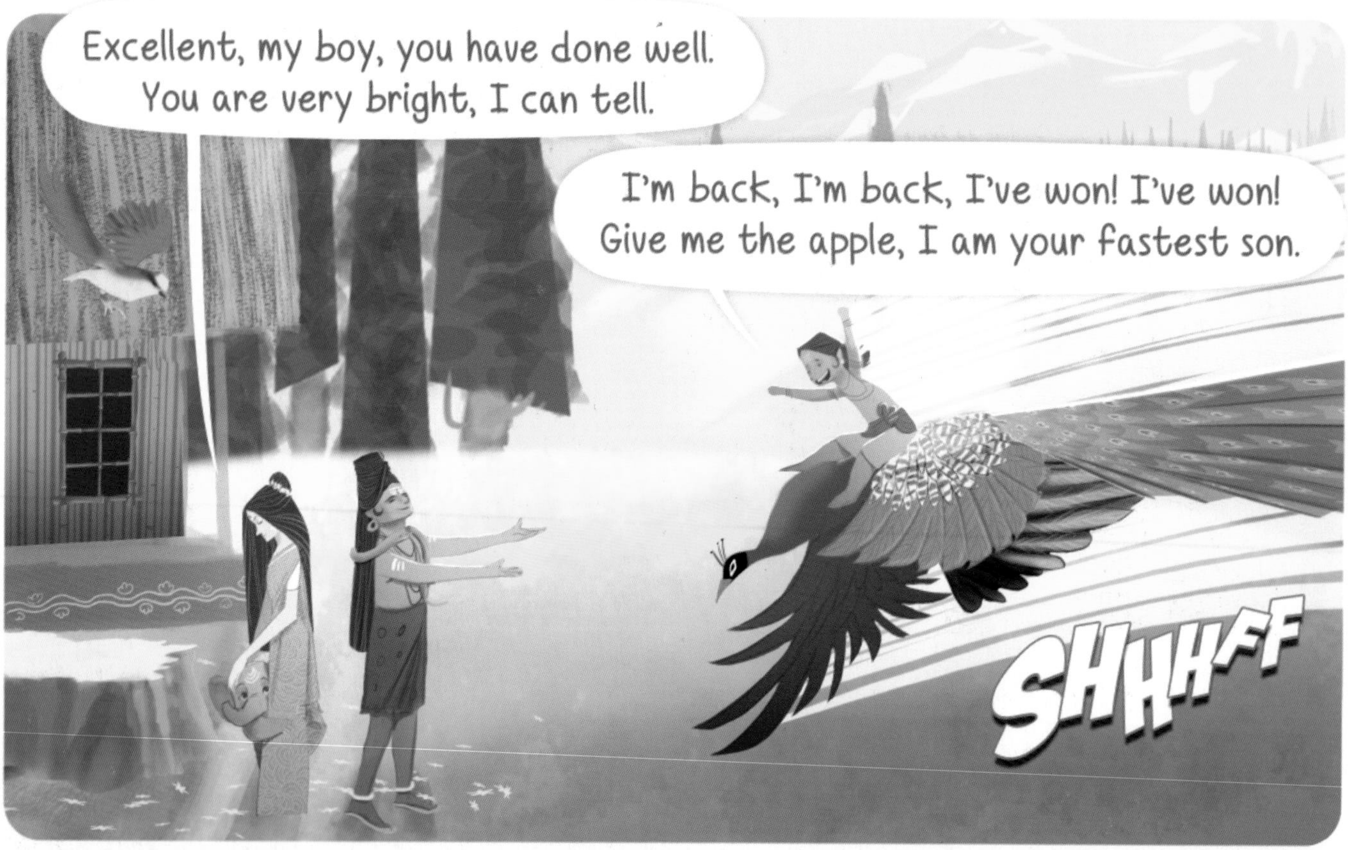
Excellent, my boy, you have done well.
You are very bright, I can tell.
I'm back, I'm back, I've won! I've won!
Give me the apple, I am your fastest son.
SHHHFF

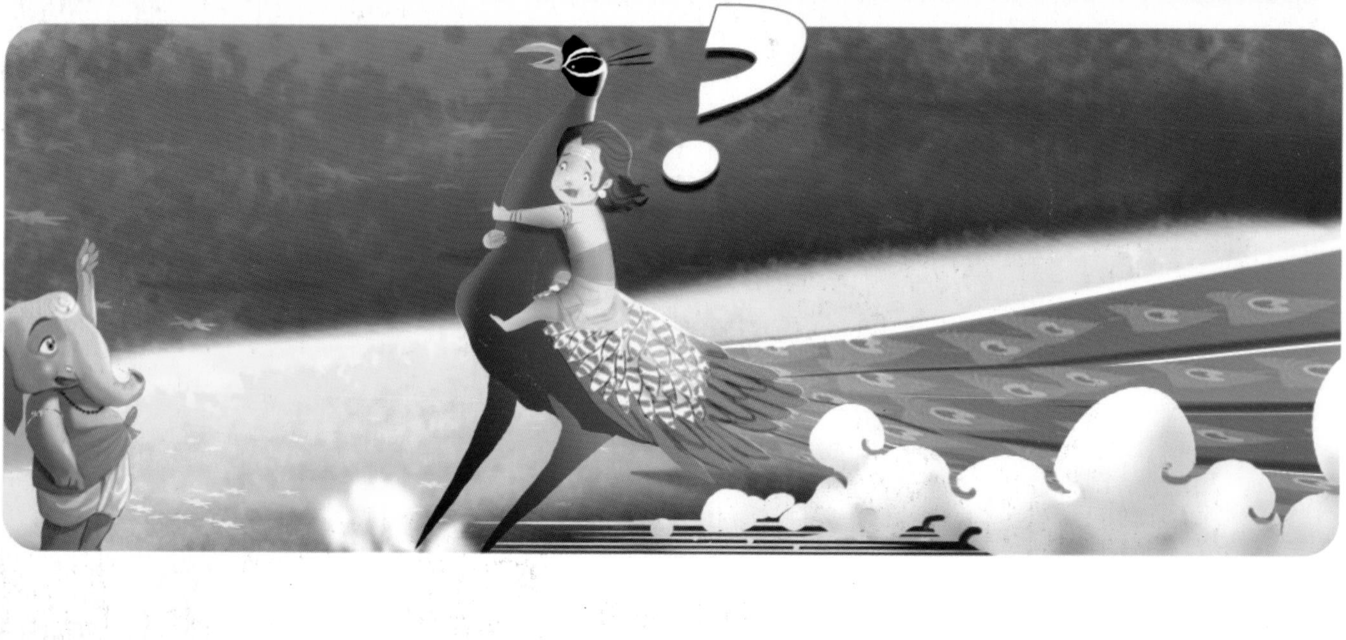
?

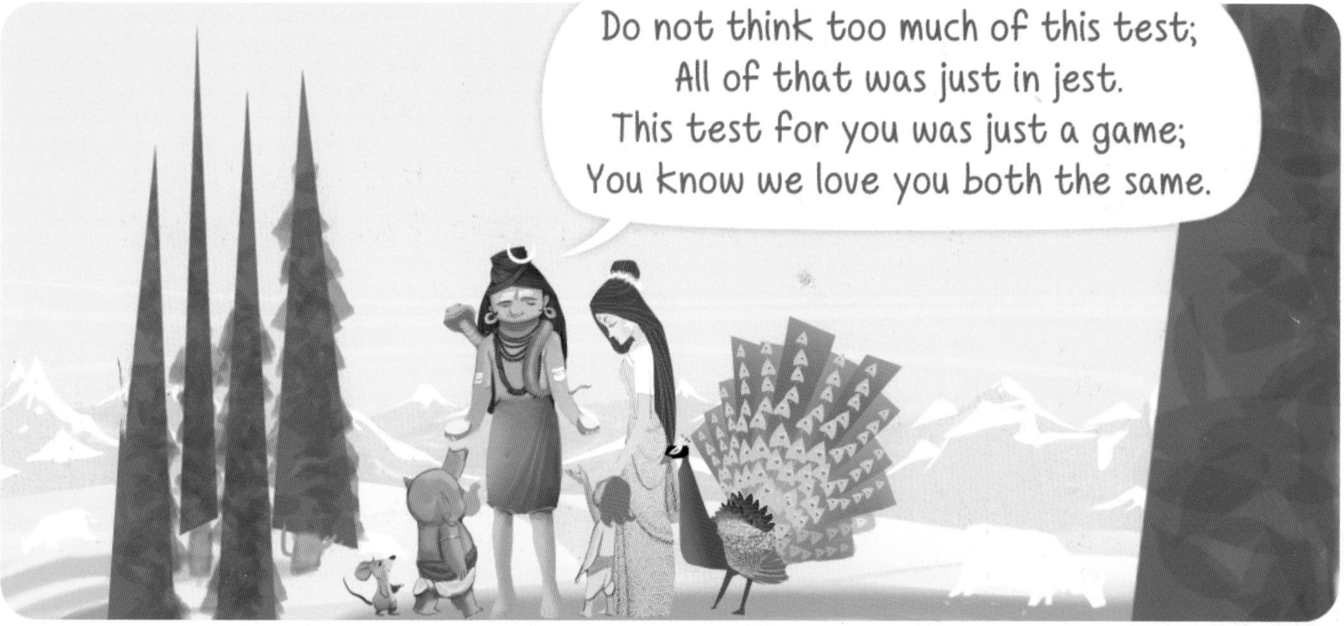
Do not think too much of this test;
All of that was just in jest.
This test for you was just a game;
You know we love you both the same.

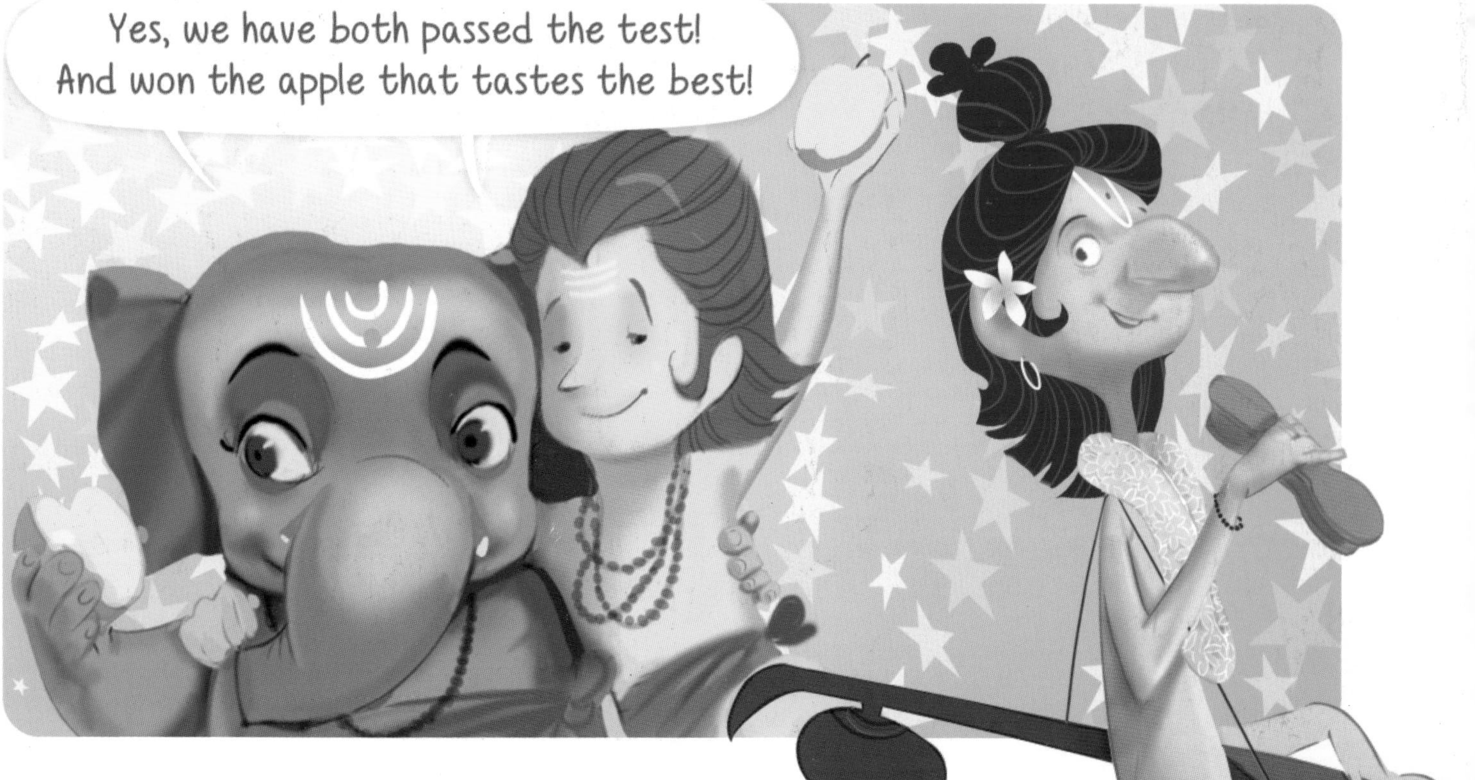
Yes, we have both passed the test!
And won the apple that tastes the best!

THE END

Ganesha and the Big Feast

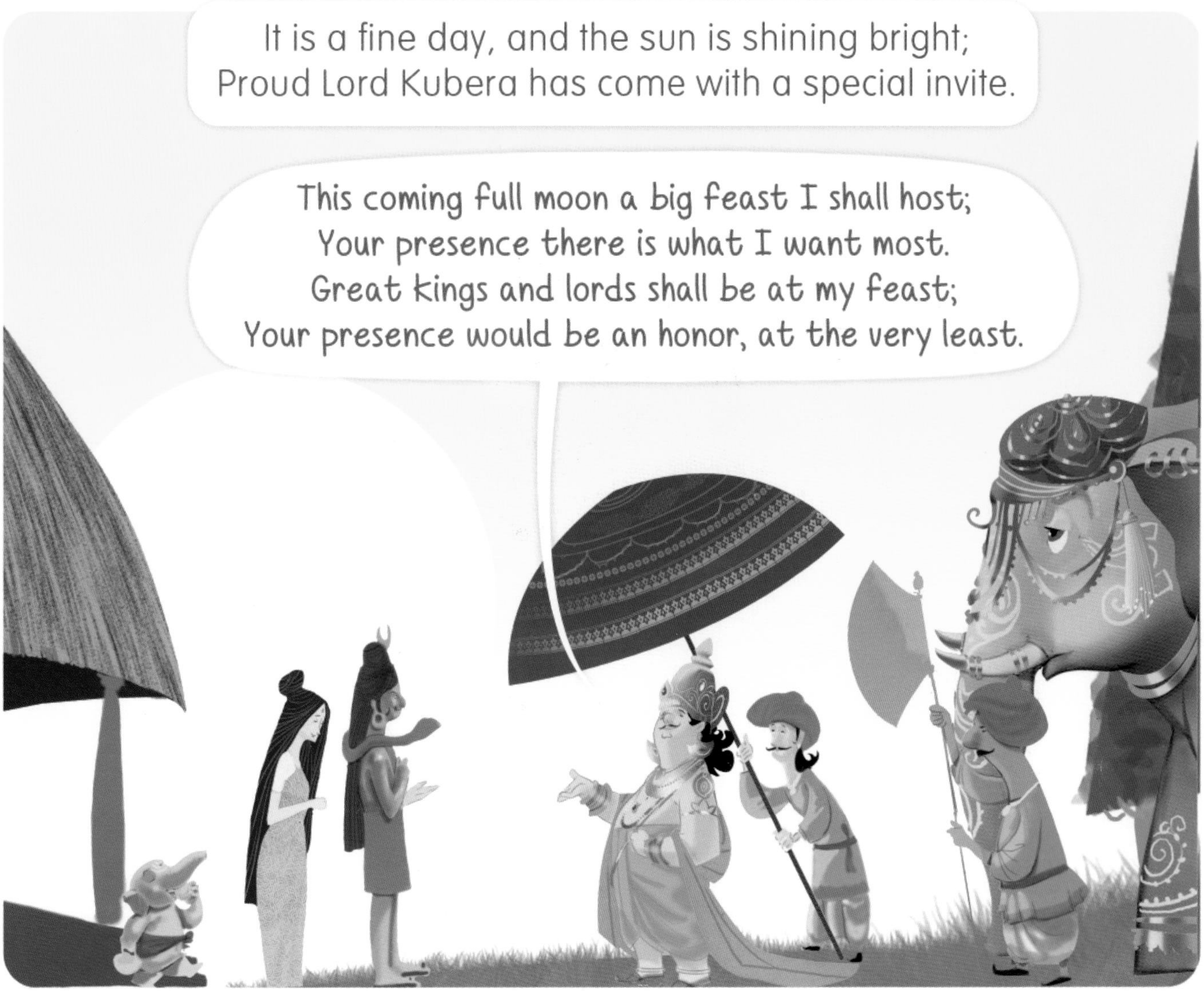
It is a fine day, and the sun is shining bright;
Proud Lord Kubera has come with a special invite.
This coming full moon a big feast I shall host;
Your presence there is what I want most.
Great kings and lords shall be at my feast;
Your presence would be an honor, at the very least.

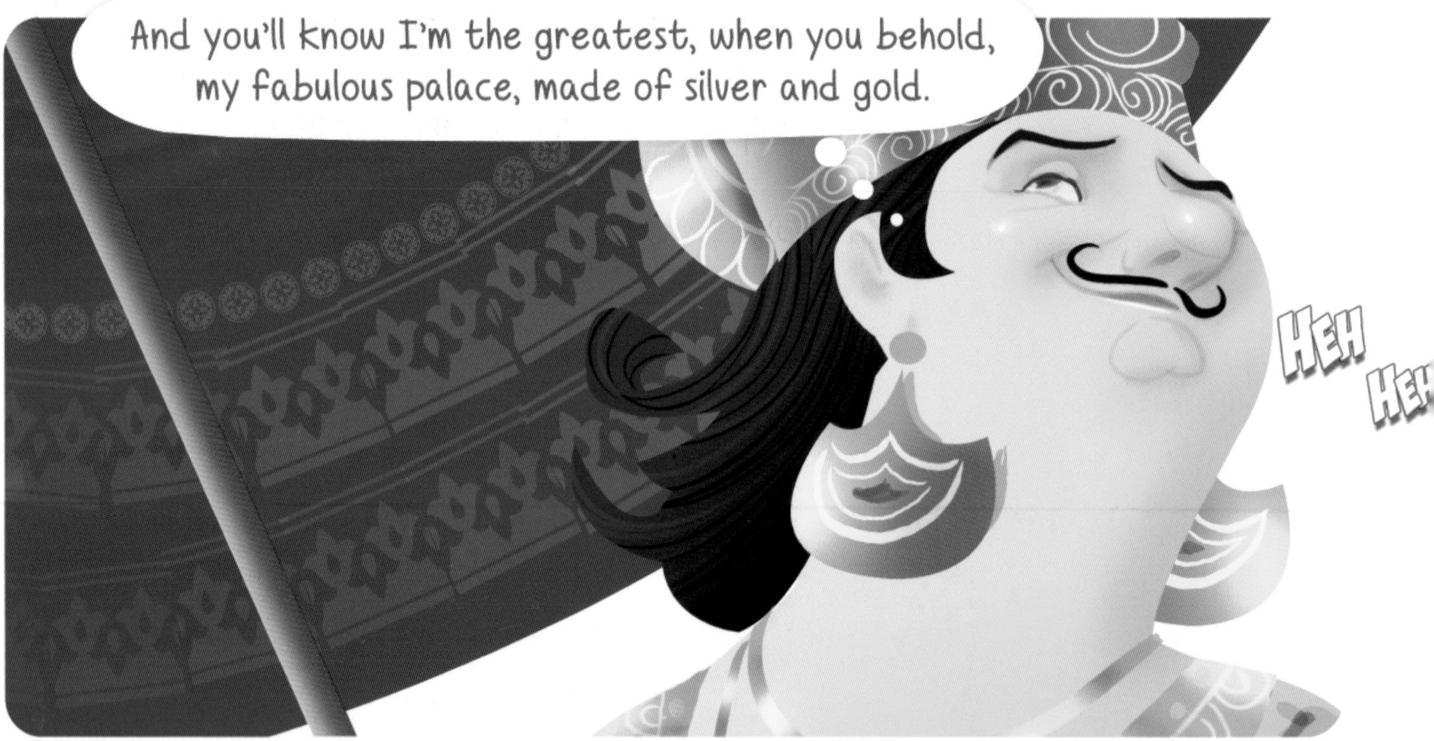
And you'll know I'm the greatest, when you behold,
my fabulous palace, made of silver and gold.
HEH
HEH

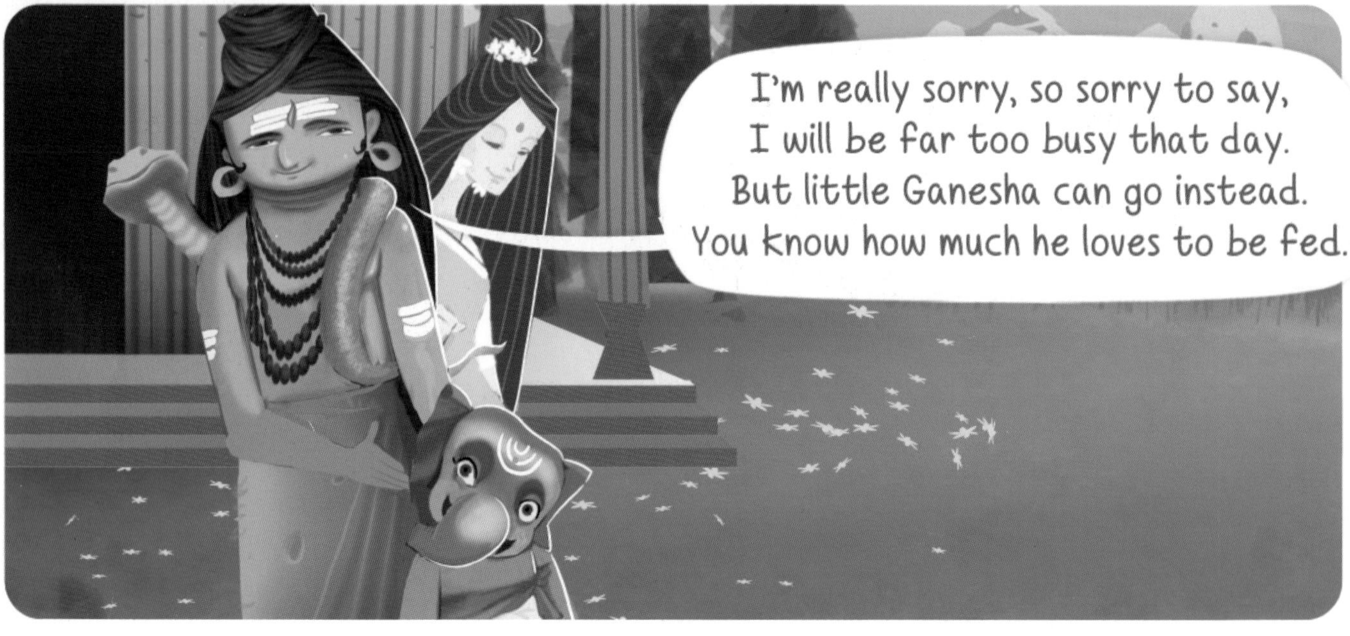
I'm really sorry, so sorry to say,
I will be far too busy that day.
But little Ganesha can go instead.
You know how much he loves to be fed.

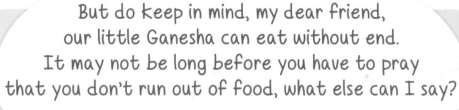

Yes, yes, I would love to go!
And eat, and eat, I would love that so!

But do keep in mind, my dear friend,
our little Ganesha can eat without end.
It may not be long before you have to pray
that you don't run out of food, what else can I say?

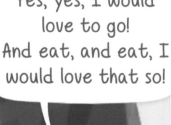

My riches are endless, and at my feast,
there'll be food from all countries, from west to east.

GRRR...

This much I can tell you, just you hear!
I will never run out of food, is that clear?

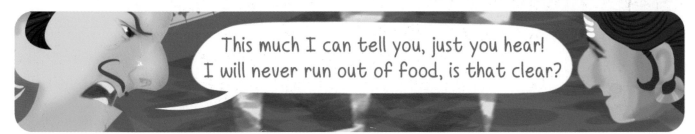

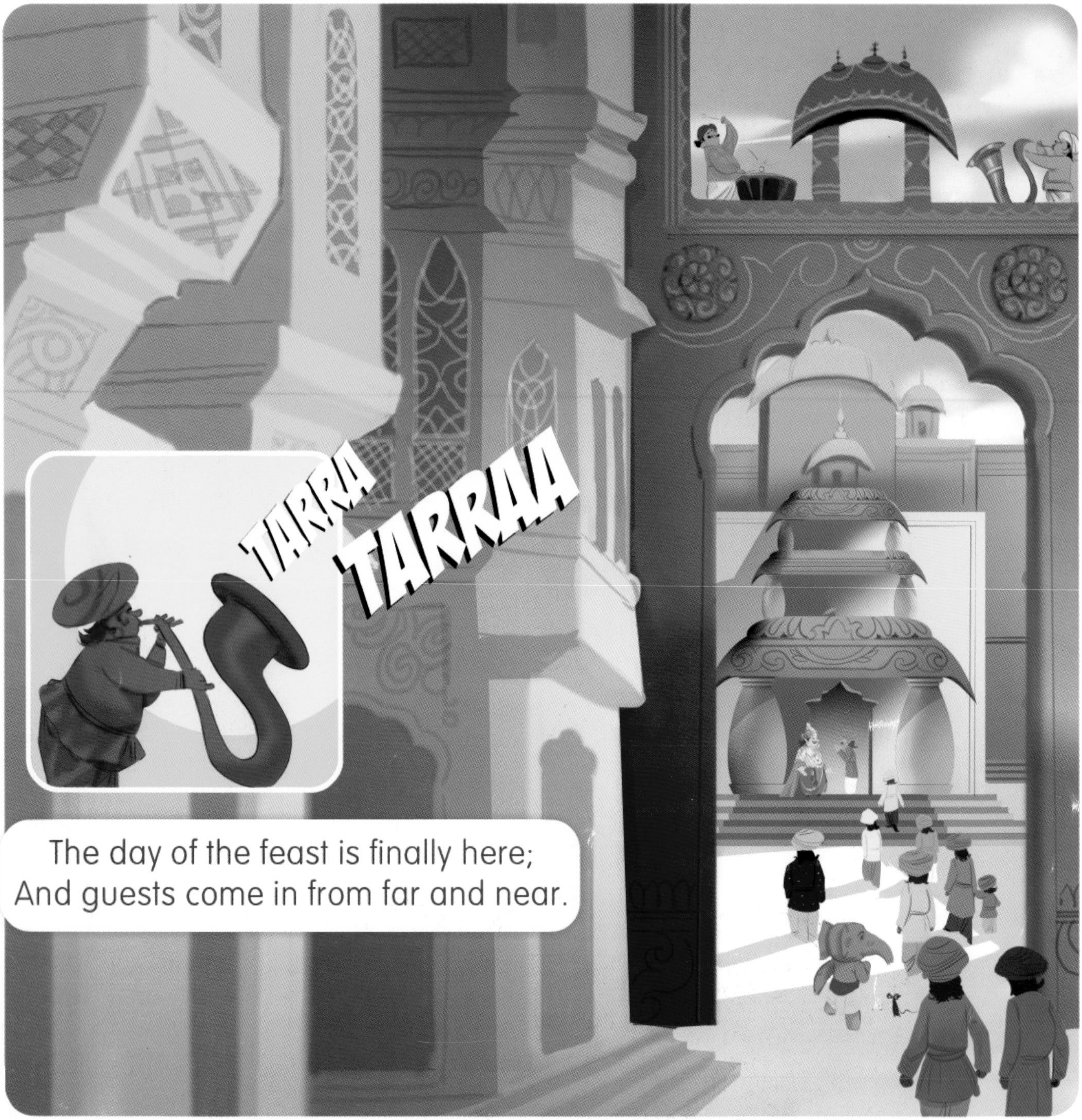
TARRA
TARRAA

The day of the feast is finally here;
And guests come in from far and near.

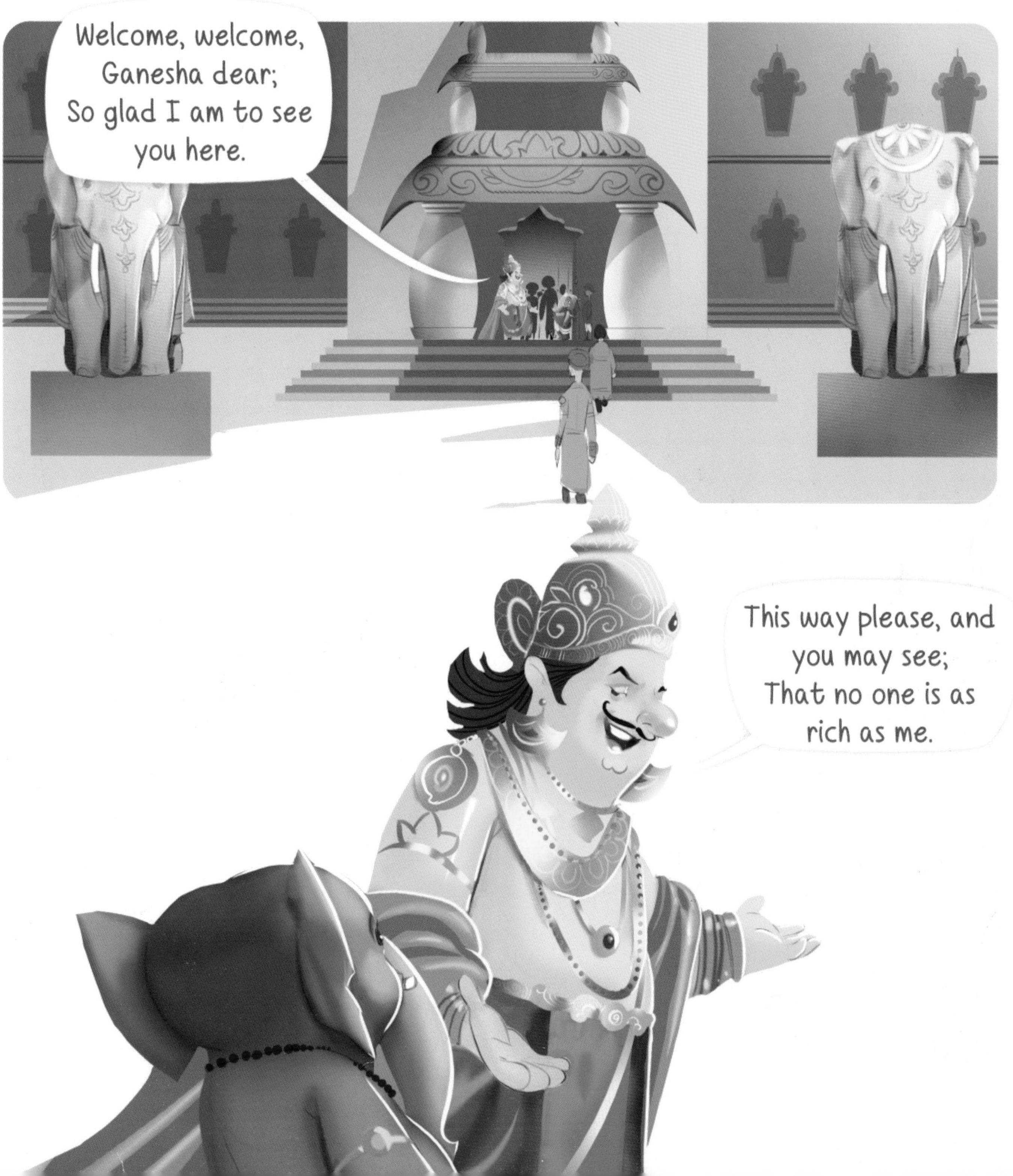
Welcome, welcome, Ganesha dear; So glad I am to see you here.
This way please, and you may see; That no one is as rich as me.

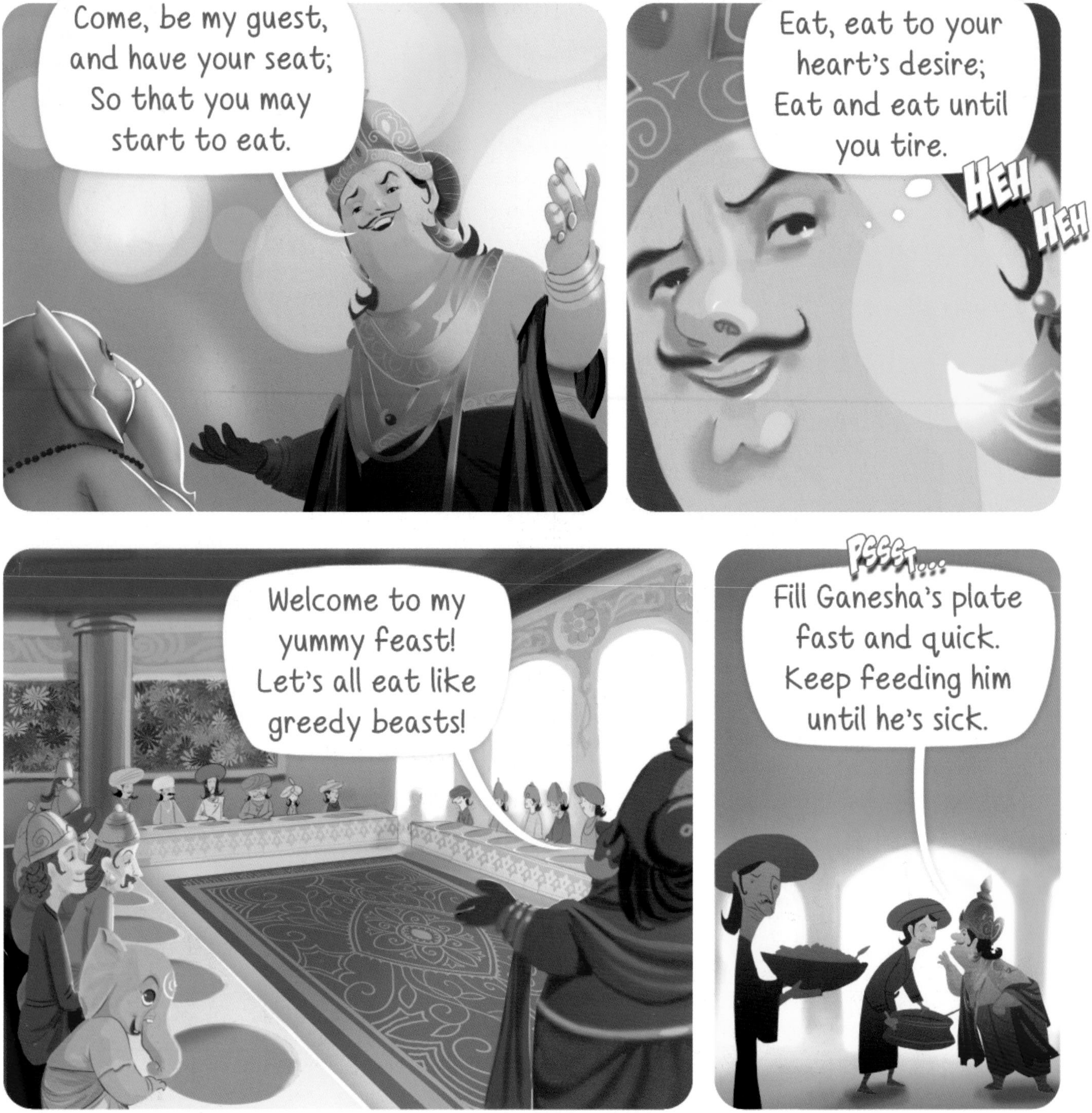
Come, be my guest, and have your seat; So that you may start to eat.
Eat, eat to your heart's desire; Eat and eat until you tire.
HEH HEH
Welcome to my yummy feast! Let's all eat like greedy beasts!
PSSST...
Fill Ganesha's plate fast and quick. Keep feeding him until he's sick.

All the guests now start to eat.
So many dishes, rich and sweet...

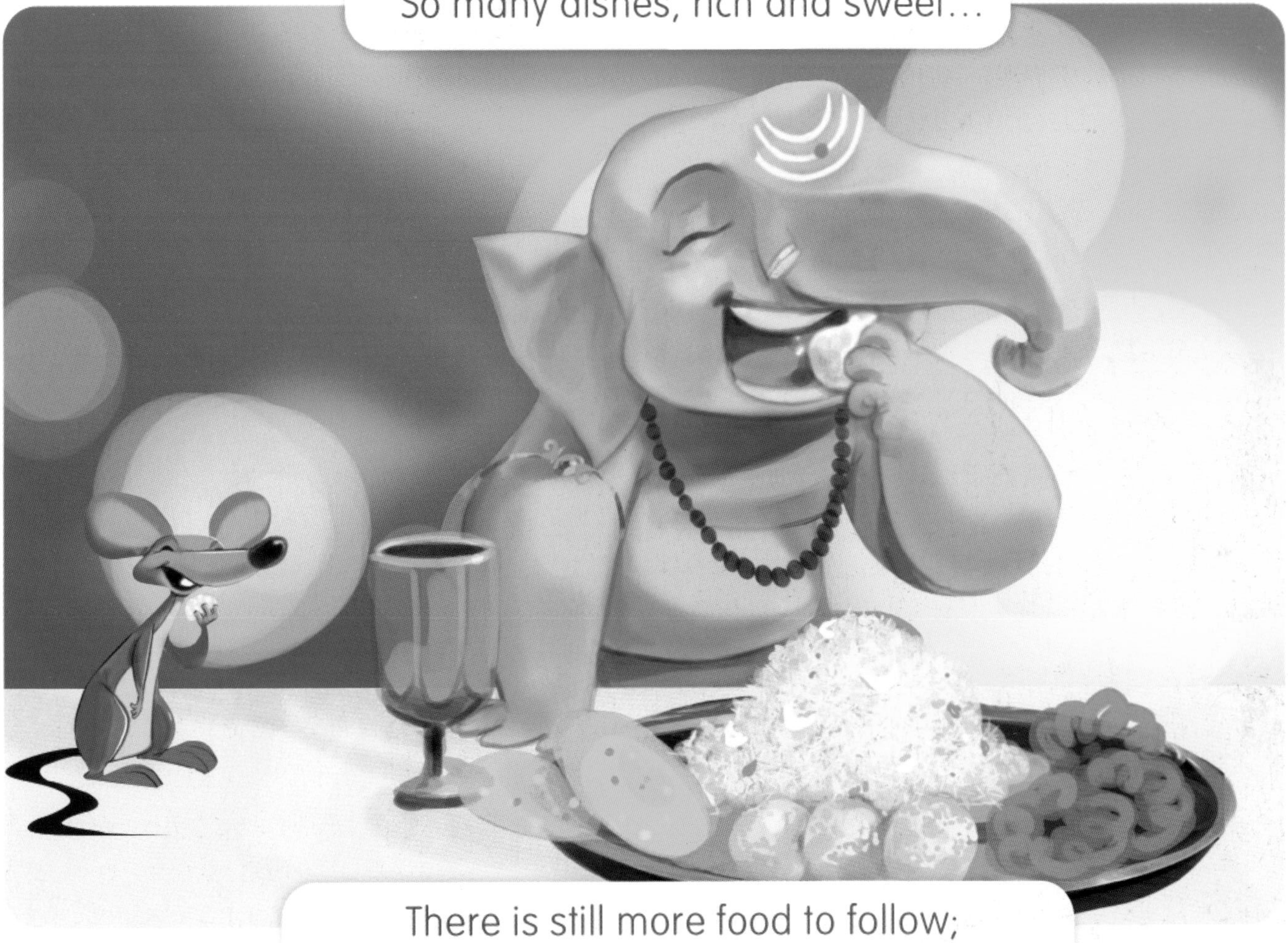

There is still more food to follow;
But see how much Ganesha can swallow...

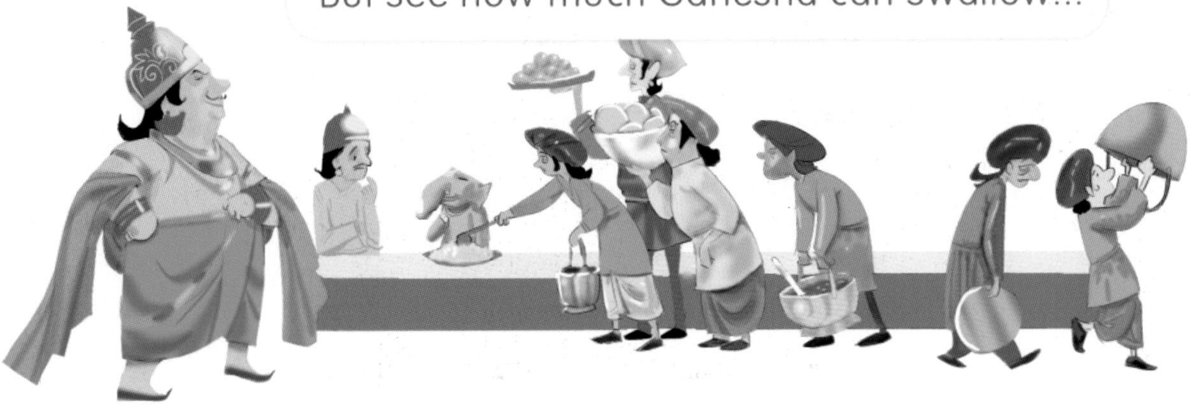

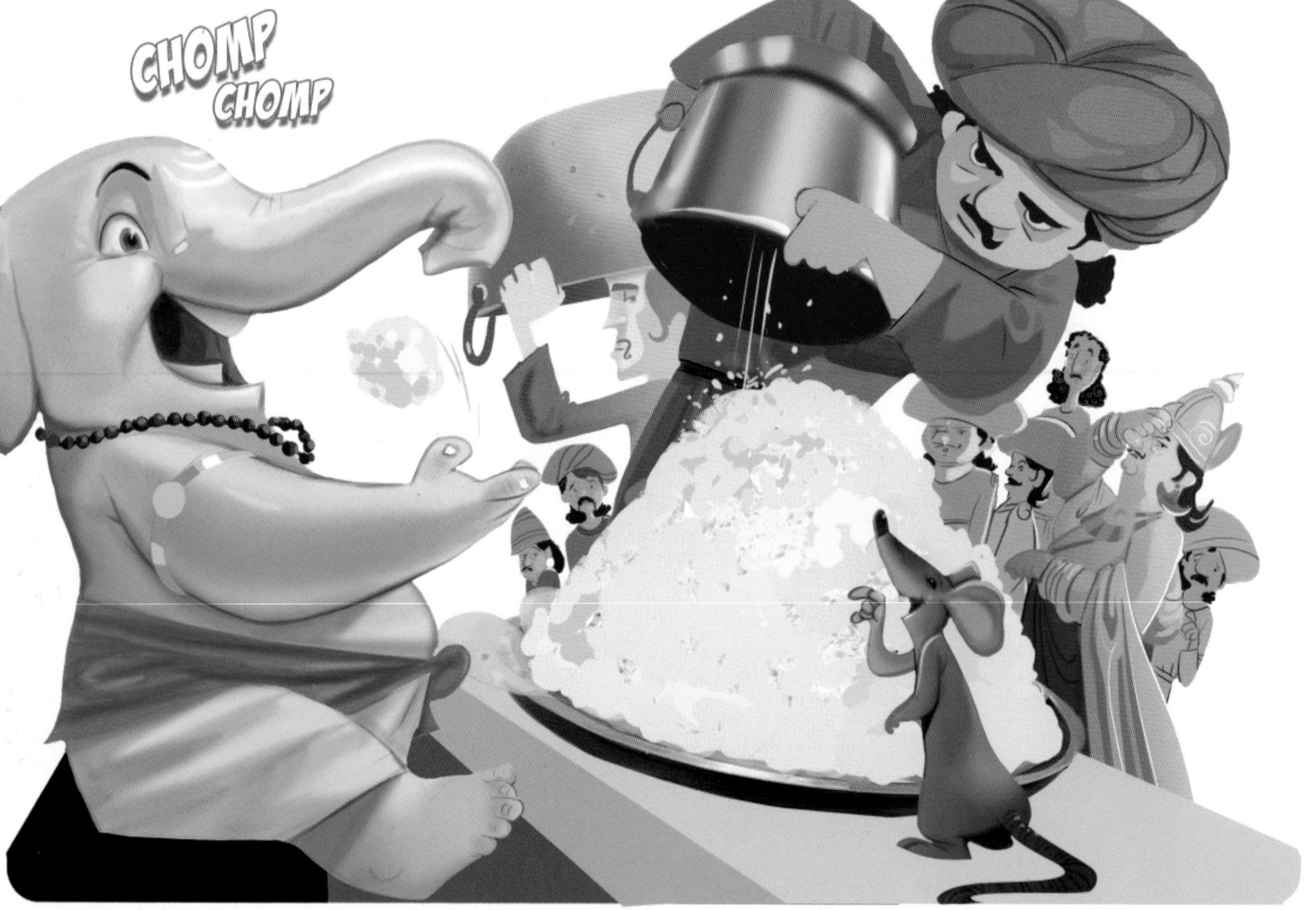
CHOMP
CHOMP

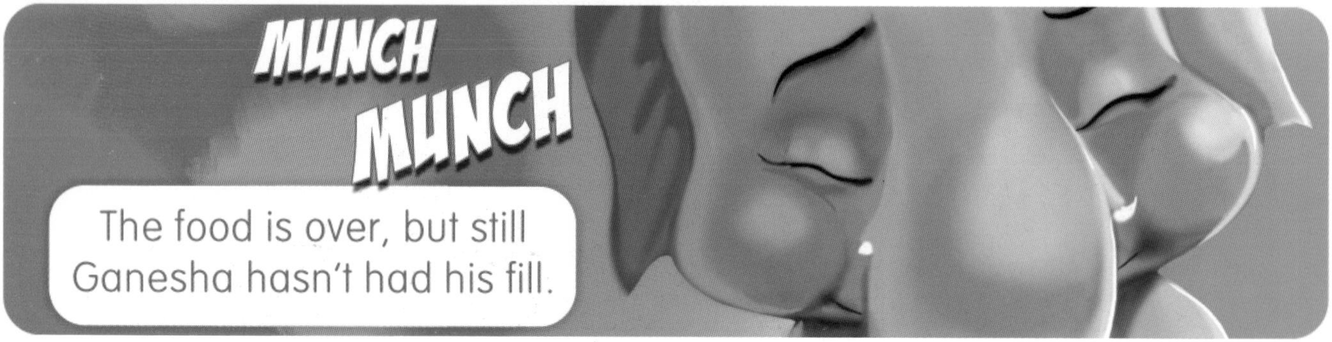
MUNCH
MUNCH
The food is over, but still
Ganesha hasn't had his fill.

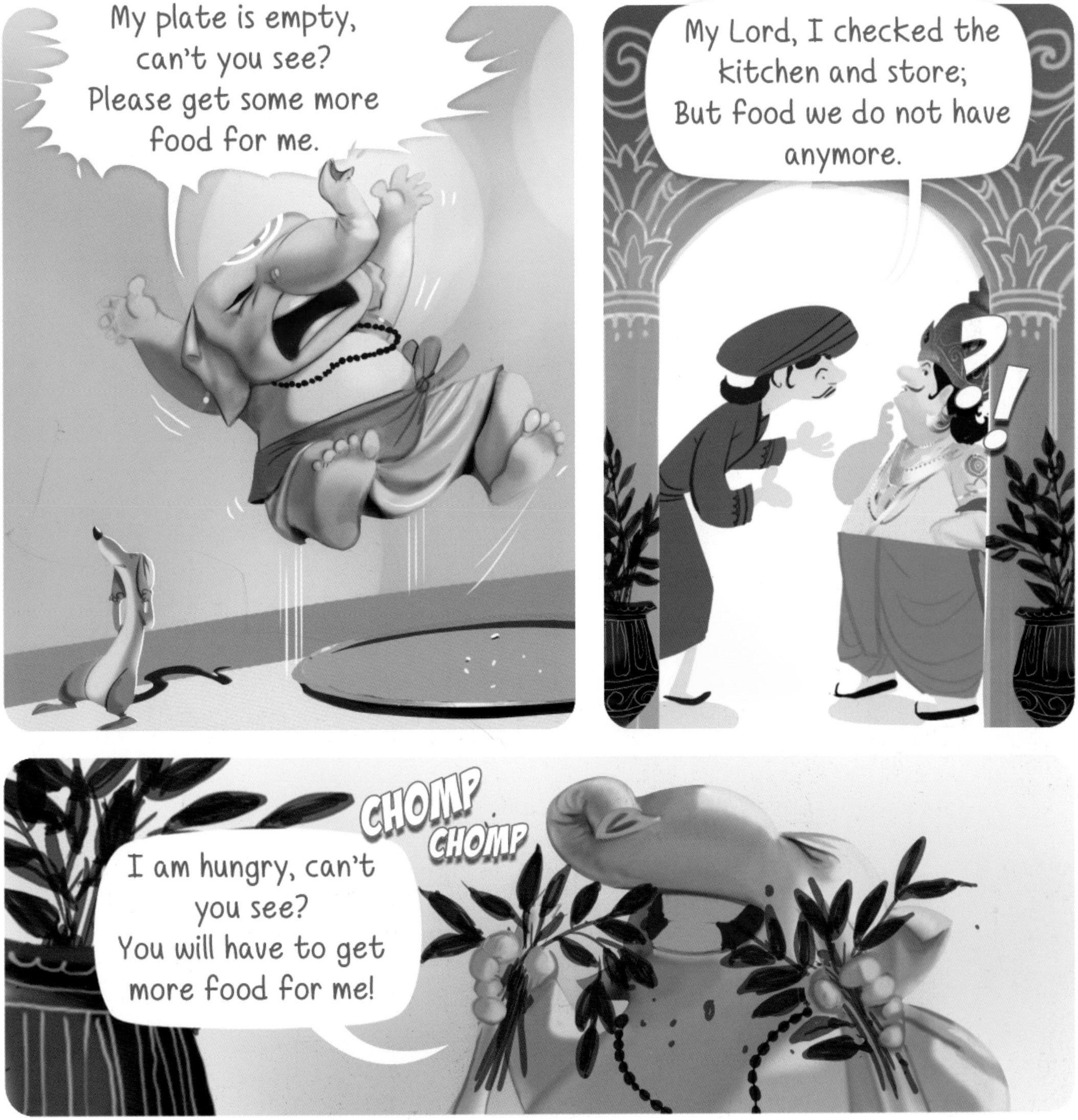
My plate is empty, can't you see? Please get some more food for me.
My Lord, I checked the kitchen and store; But food we do not have anymore.
CHOMP
CHOMP
I am hungry, can't you see? You will have to get more food for me!

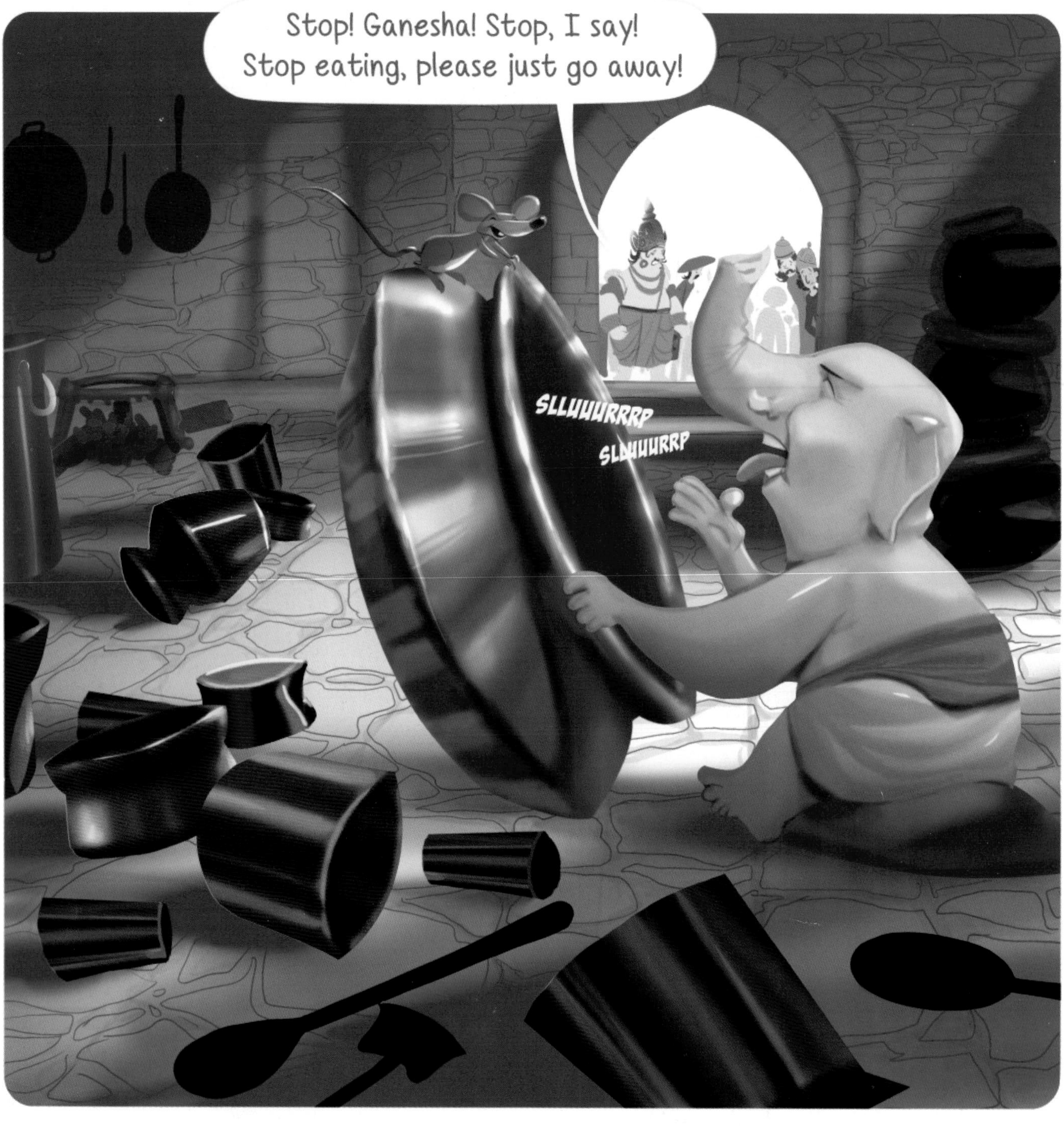
Stop! Ganesha! Stop, I say! Stop eating, please just go away!
SLLUUURRRP
SLUUUURRP

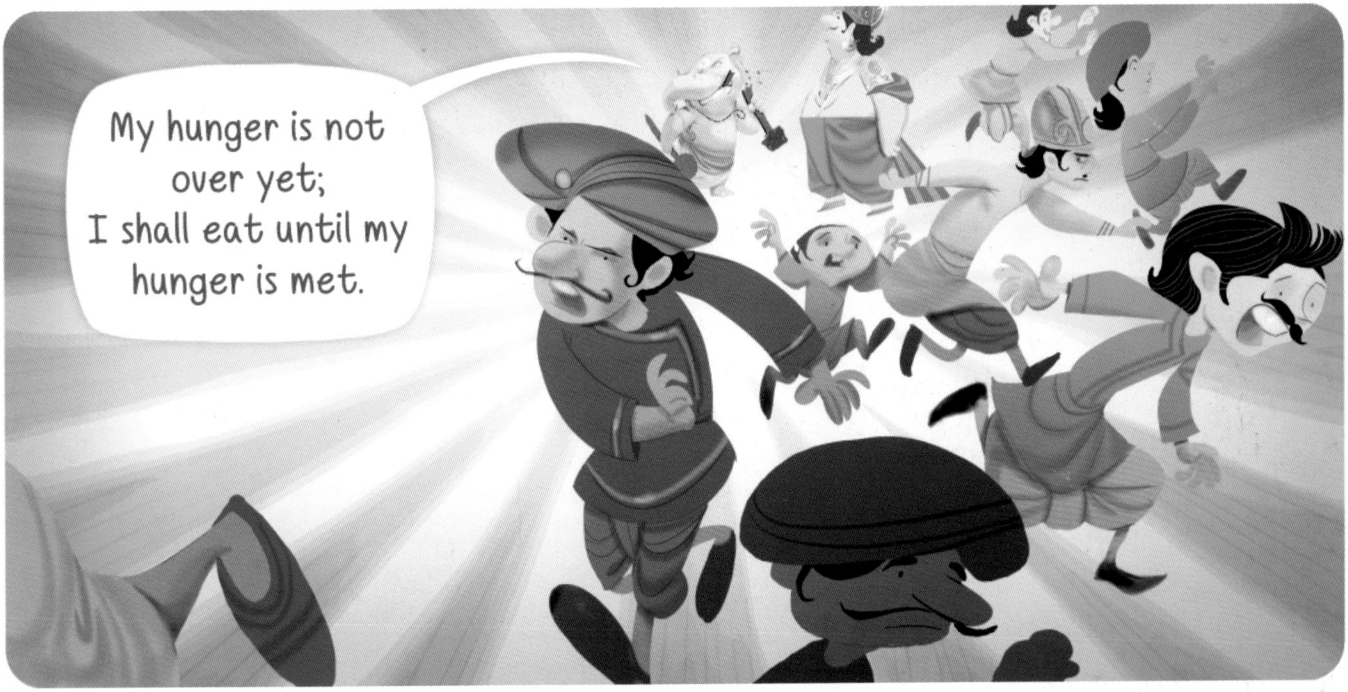
My hunger is not over yet;
I shall eat until my hunger is met.

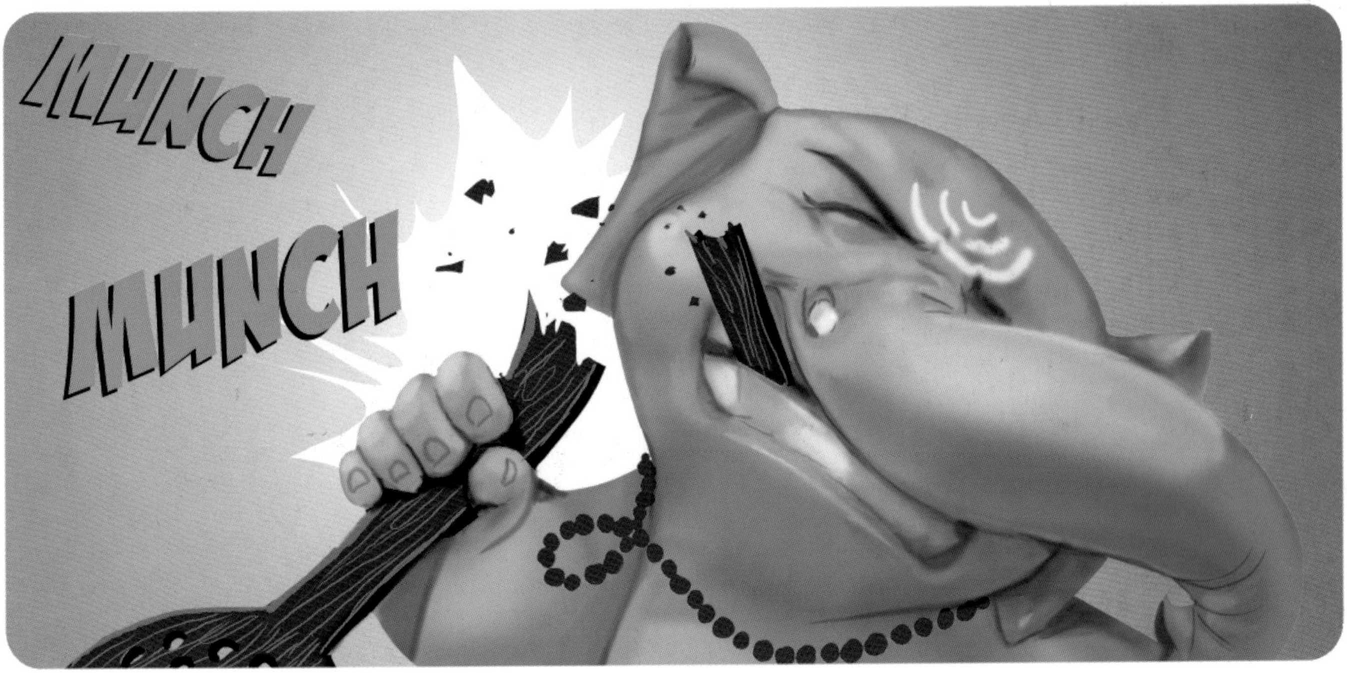
MUNCH
MUNCH

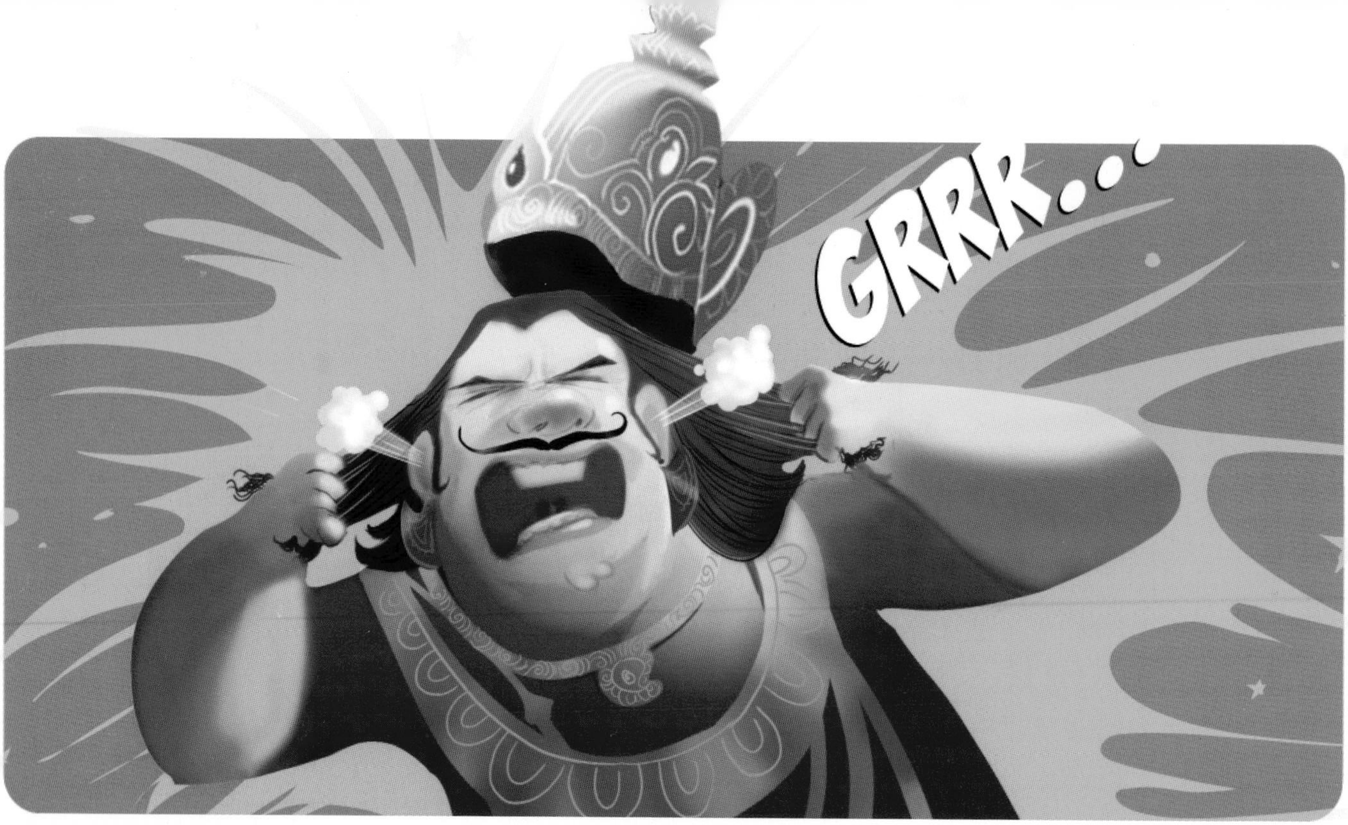
GRRR...

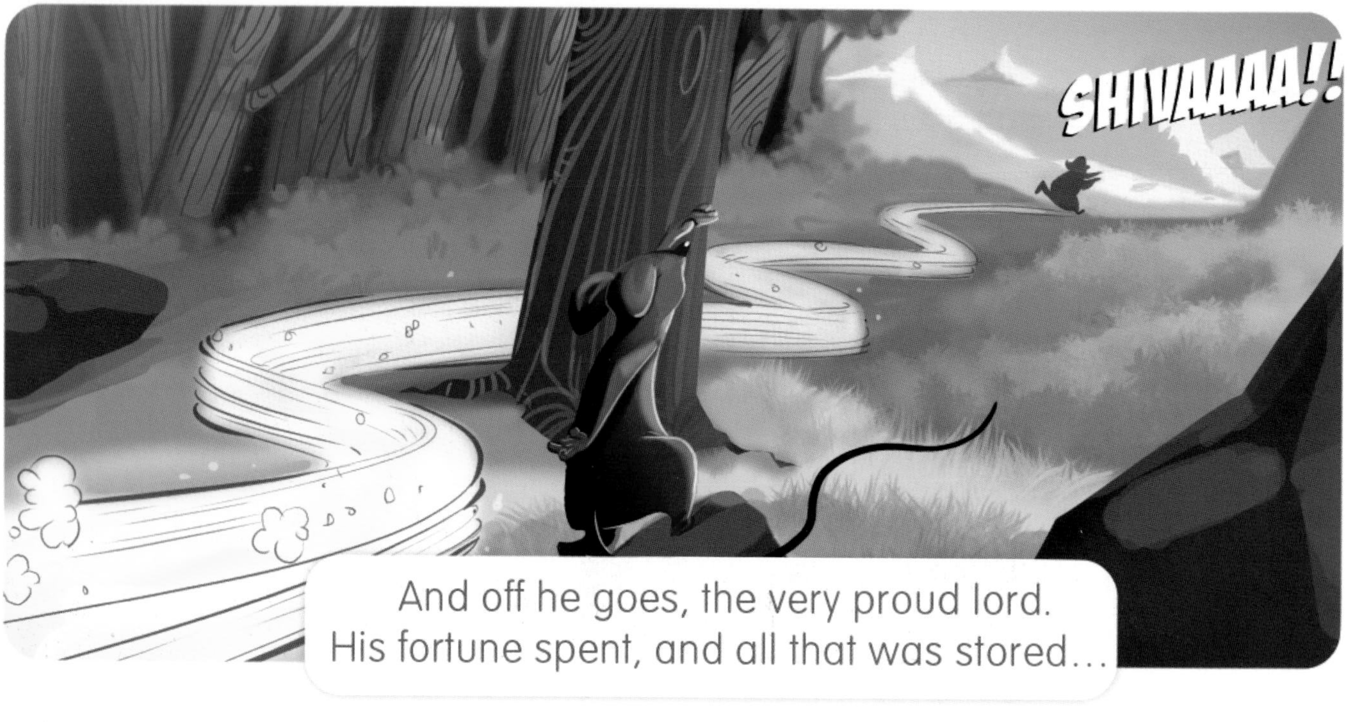
SHIVAAAA!!
And off he goes, the very proud lord.
His fortune spent, and all that was stored...

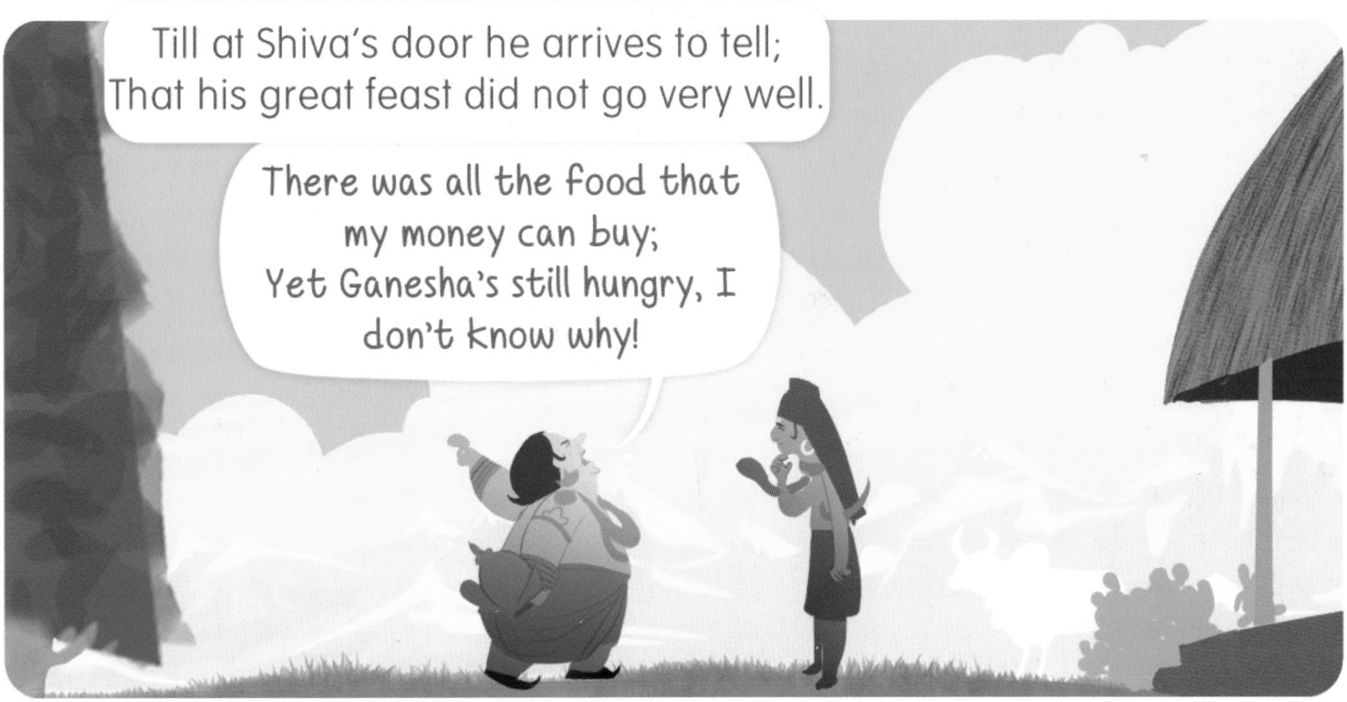
Till at Shiva's door he arrives to tell;
That his great feast did not go very well.
There was all the food that my money can buy; Yet Ganesha's still hungry, I don't know why!

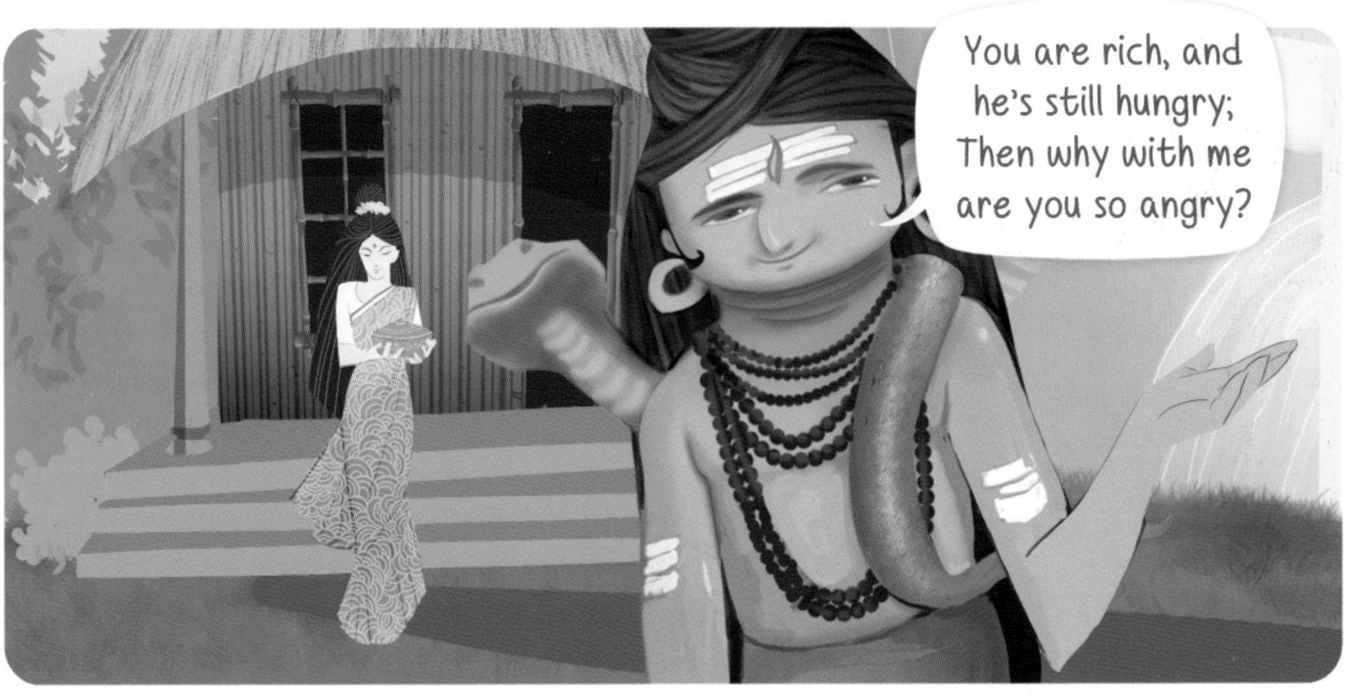
You are rich, and he's still hungry; Then why with me are you so angry?

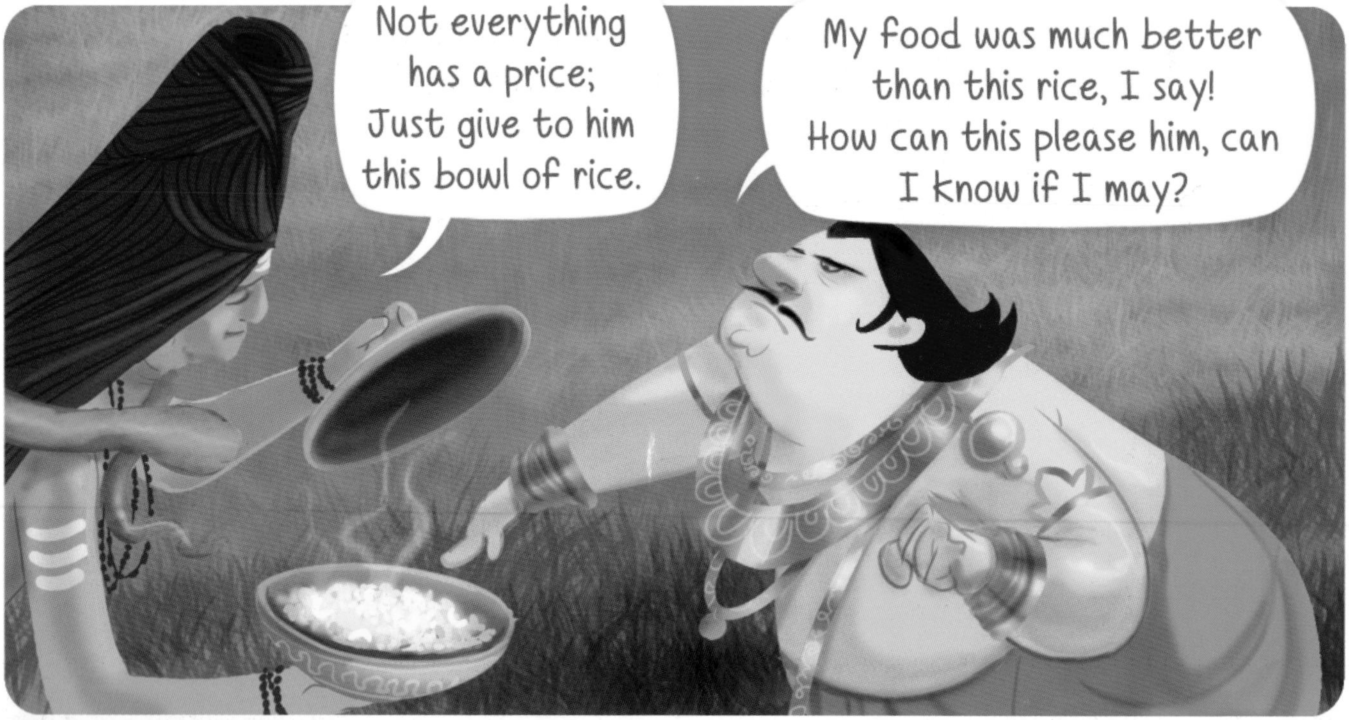
Not everything has a price; Just give to him this bowl of rice.
My food was much better than this rice, I say! How can this please him, can I know if I may?

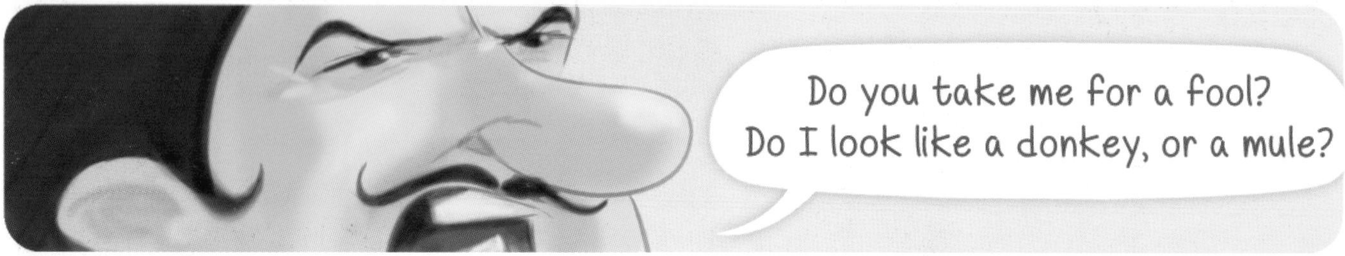
Do you take me for a fool? Do I look like a donkey, or a mule?

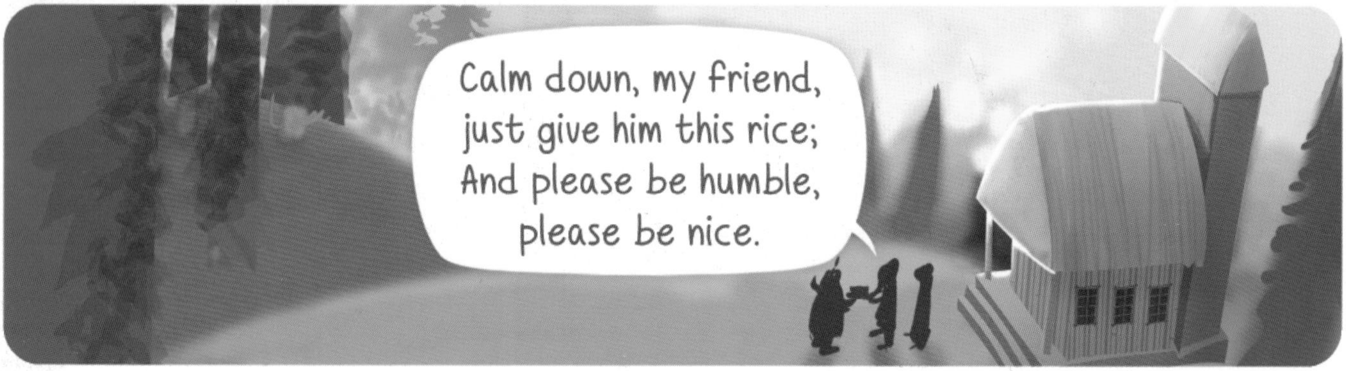
Calm down, my friend, just give him this rice; And please be humble, please be nice.

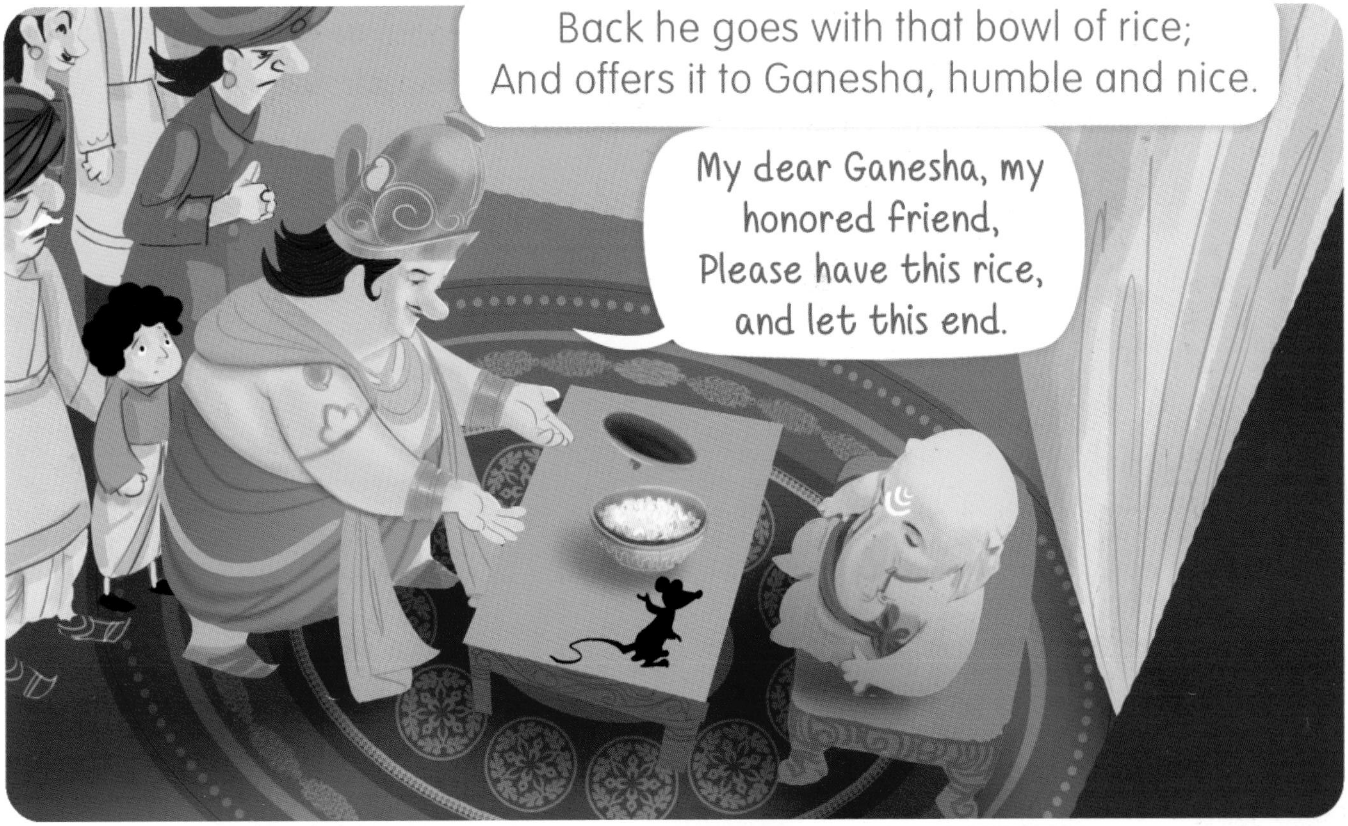
Back he goes with that bowl of rice;
And offers it to Ganesha, humble and nice.
My dear Ganesha, my honored friend, Please have this rice, and let this end.

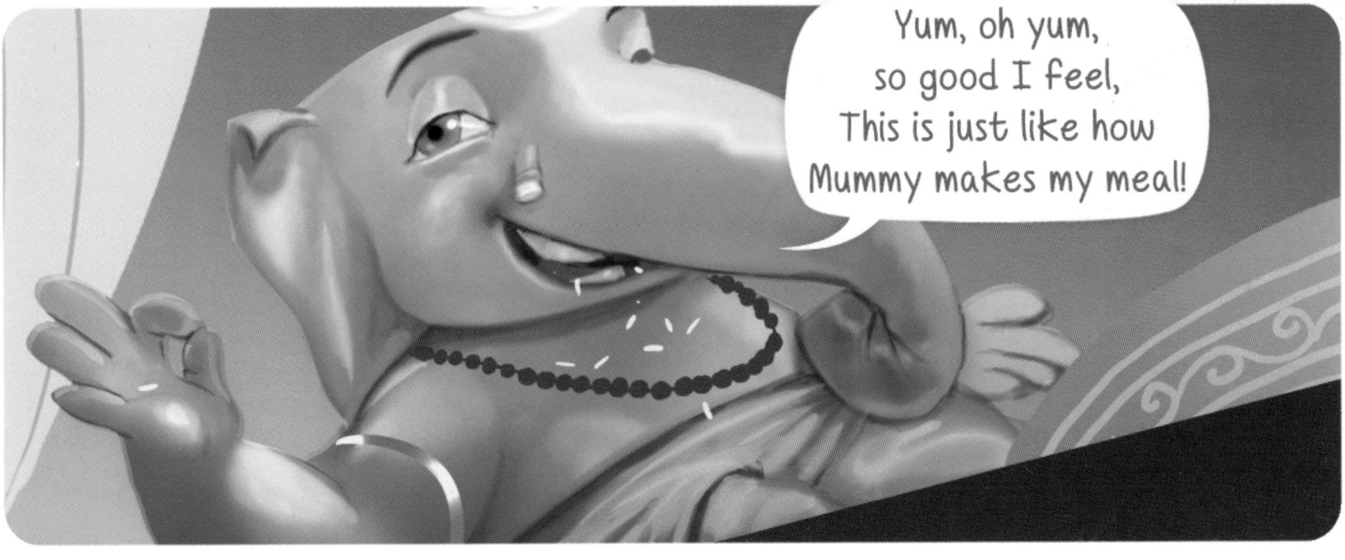
Yum, oh yum, so good I feel, This is just like how Mummy makes my meal!

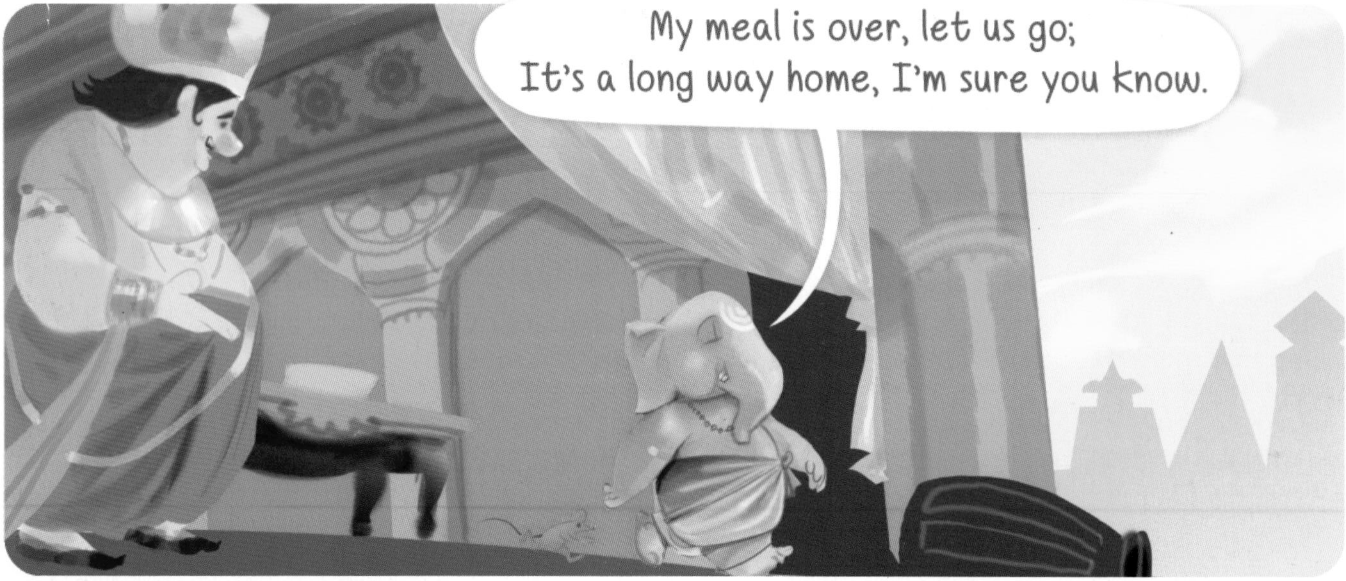
My meal is over, let us go;
It's a long way home, I'm sure you know.

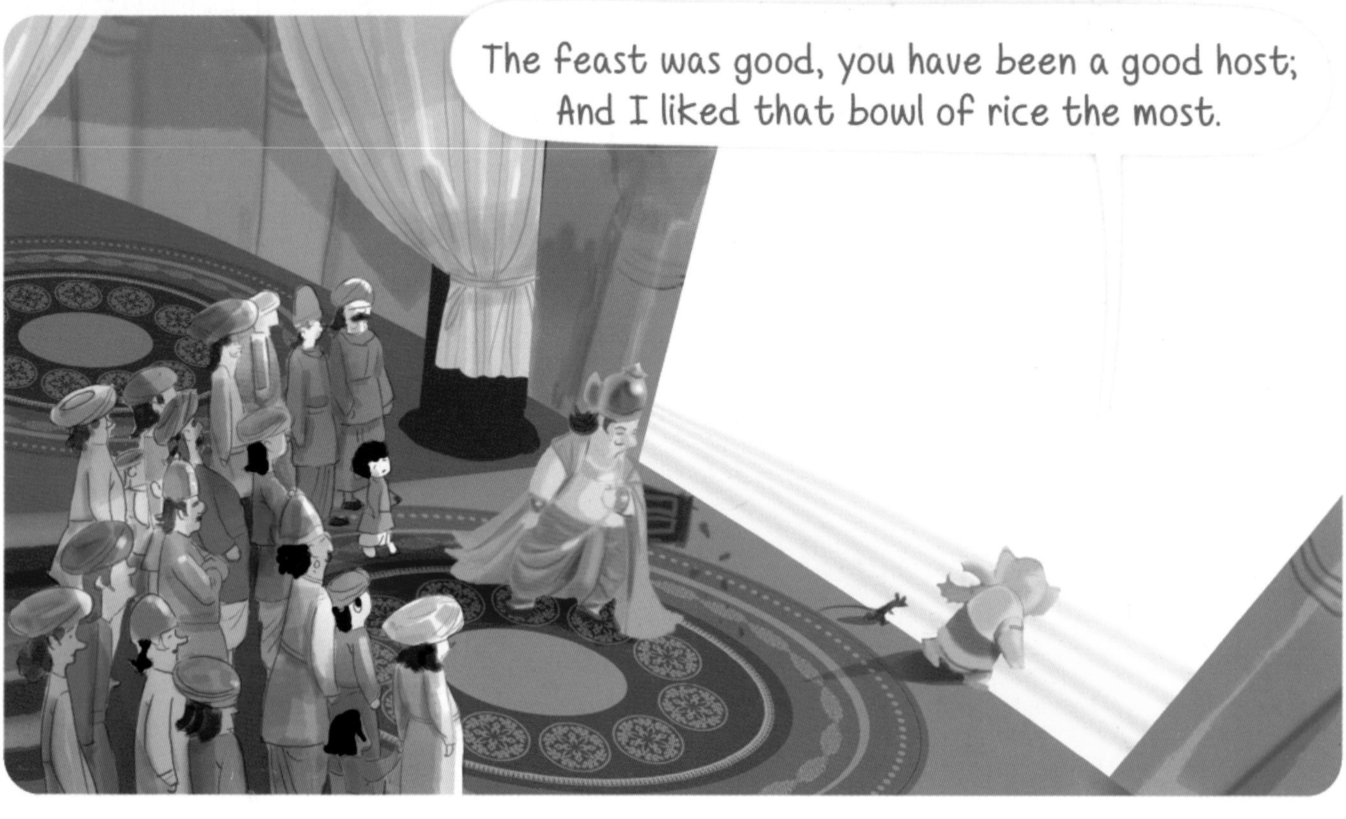
The feast was good, you have been a good host;
And I liked that bowl of rice the most.

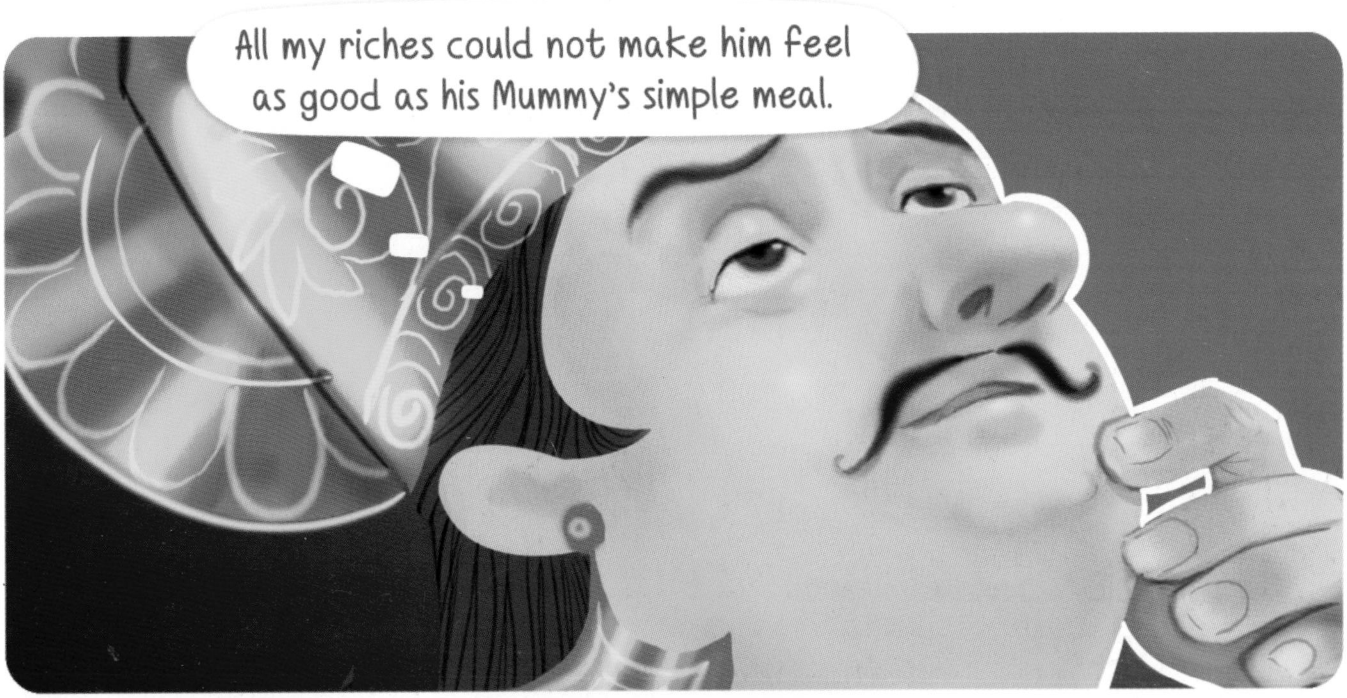
All my riches could not make him feel as good as his Mummy's simple meal.

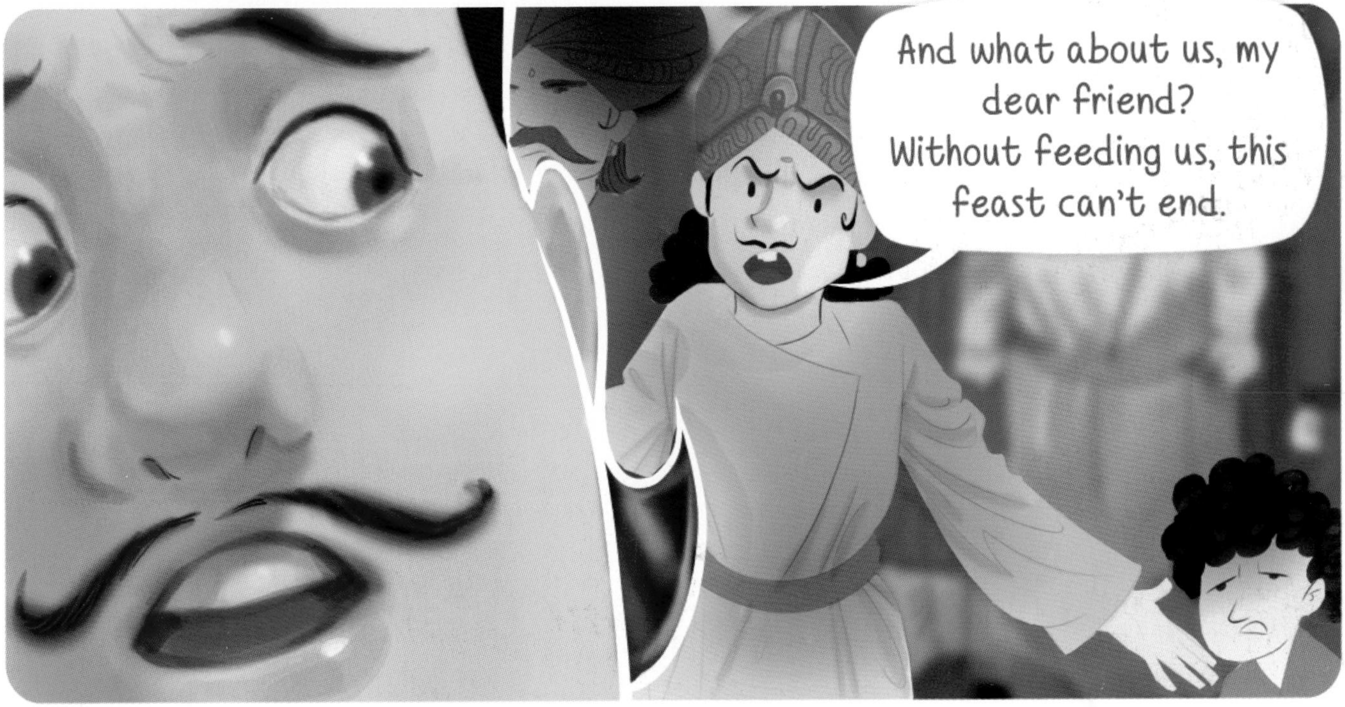
And what about us, my dear friend? Without feeding us, this feast can't end.

NOT THE END

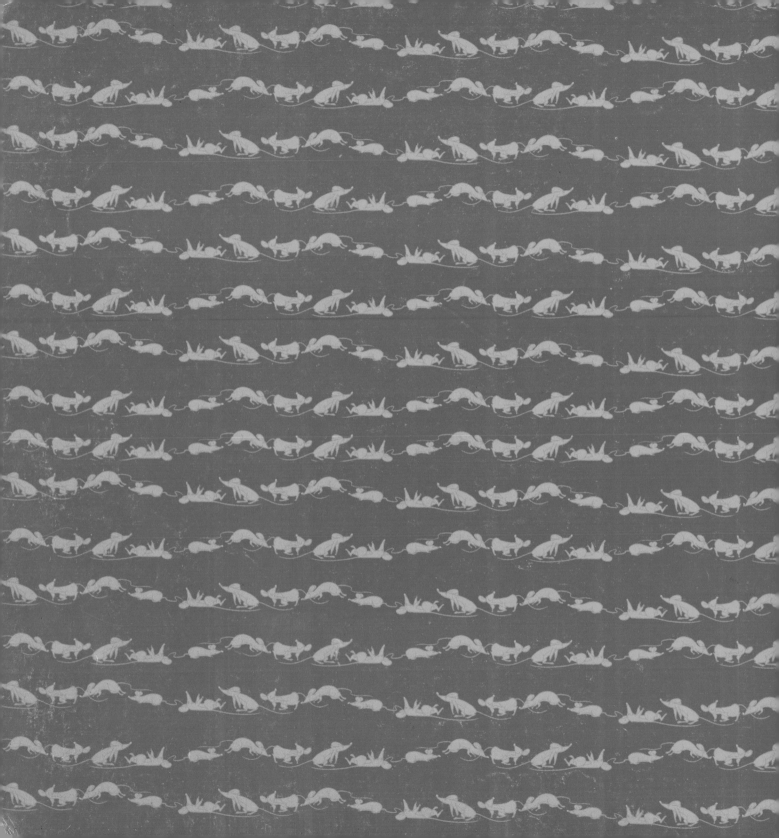